# AND ACKNOWLEDGEMENTS

This one goes out to the man who inspires my wandering mind and busy fingers. DH, this one is for you!

This version of THE GIFT is an updated and re-released version of the novel originally published by Etopia Press. Without their call for submission, I would never have written this story.

Thanks to my critique partners who had the guts to tell me where I went wrong and how to fix it.

Any mistakes in this book are mine and mine alone. I blame nobody but myself.

# CHAPTER ONE

Nick watched his wife wiggle in her seat in the back of the taxi. It was only mid-November, but tonight had been his company's Christmas party. A few years ago, his employer had started holding it early to reduce the holiday party load. It was a little untraditional, but Nick always enjoyed an evening of socializing and visiting with friends. So did his wife.

Sammy had consumed a fair amount of wine with her dinner and followed up with a couple of spiced rum and ginger ales. She wasn't drunk by a long stretch, but she was definitely in a good mood and more than a bit horny. The evening had been long, the company and food fabulous. He smiled, remembering the way she had wiggled and danced to the music of the band. She loved music and dancing. Nick loved the way alcohol and dancing combined to turn his wife into a horny little minx. He leaned against the corner of the door, watching her, and noticed the cabbie was having trouble keeping his eyes off her.

She wiggled and twisted, and he knew she was doing it deliberately to turn him on. Knowing the driver was watching just added fuel to her fire. Her blue eyes flashed, and her curly blonde hair was starting to come undone from its fancy up-do. She had a sexy, come hither, I need fucked look, and it was driving Nick to distraction.

She hadn't always been like this. Nick recalled their college days when they had first met. Sammy had been hot, but unsure of her sexuality and very inexperienced. It was this combination that had first attracted him to her. One look at her hot body and her shy smile and he was a goner. He knew instantly that she was going to become very important in his life. He just hadn't realized she would become his wife.

Tonight he recalled their first few dates with a smile and an almost gleeful mental rubbing of his hands to think of the sexy siren she had become. She had grown from a shy almost-virgin to a red-hot mama, and it was all for him. She dressed sexily, coming close to sleazy when they went out, but she never quite crossed the line to tramp. She simply looked hot. He had overheard a couple men at the party talking about wanting her, and it only made Nick want her more.

They pulled up in front of their house, and Sammy shimmied to the front of the seat, her skirt sliding up to reveal the full length of her toned legs. She leaned forward to thank the driver, giving him a hot, sexy smile and a full view of the sexy red bra covering her generous breasts.

Nick almost laughed when the man knocked ten dollars off the cost of the ride. He paid the man, tipped him generously, and followed Sammy's wiggling ass into the house. Ten minutes later, Sammy unceremoniously stripped him of his clothing and pushed him backward onto the bed. She pulled off her dress, slipped out of her panties, and kneeled over him.

"I've decided what I want for Christmas." Sammy eased herself down on her husband's long, thick cock. Allowing just the head to slip inside her, she paused, her legs burning with the effort it took to hold herself perched in a squat above him without sheathing him fully inside and grinding against him. She wiggled back and forth a bit, her small motions threatening to dislodge him. "I don't want you to buy me a gift." She wiggled again. "Instead, I want you to do something for me."

"Ah, is this really the time to ask a favor?" He growled up at her, tugging on her hips in a vain attempt to draw her down onto his hardness. After two weeks out of town on a project, he was near to bursting with need. "Come on," he pleaded, "slide down onto me."

*The Gift* 4

Compliant for a second, she eased another inch inside herself, biting her lip to keep her own arousal at bay. This wouldn't work if she gave in now and let him have what they both needed so badly. She had to stay strong and resist the urge to take him hard, right now.

"I want you to do something for me," she repeated, easing upward, allowing his erection to slip until she was hovering with him barely broaching her entrance. "Come on, Nick, tell me you'll do this—" Her words were a plea and a demand all at once. Come on, dammit, agree before I orgasm and lose my power over you. She wiggled a little, her hands coming up to cup her breasts, fingers kneading and tweaking her nipples. She pushed up on her breasts, pushing them over the top of her bra. She pulled a little, stretching her breasts toward him in the way that always drove him wild.

Nick groaned and reached up to cup her breasts himself. Sammy eased away from him and waggled her finger. "Nothing for you until you agree…" She trailed off enticingly, swiveling her hips, her hands tangling in her blonde curls and messing her hair sexily.

"Dammit, Sammy," he swore up at her. "I've been waiting for this for weeks." He bucked upward, trying to seat himself deeper within her hot wetness.

Sammy felt his cock throbbing and knew he was almost beyond waiting any longer. She knew how badly he needed her, almost desperately. Since their first date three years ago, they had had sex almost every night. This had been their longest dry spell since their wedding. Working out of town and away from your woman was hell when you had a high sex drive like his. He had only been back in town for an hour before they had to leave for the party.

She tsked at him, grabbed his hands and, leaning forward, pulled them to rest on the bed above his head. "I've been waiting too, and I've been a good girl." She smiled a naughty smile as she dragged her breasts across his face, careful to keep them clear of his questing mouth. "I didn't even make myself come. Not even once." Her face colored. "Well, except for that time on the phone with you. We'll have to do that again sometime." She smiled fondly at the memory of their first phone sex. Slowly easing another inch of his rock hard cock into her drenched pussy, she added, "but not tonight."

"Come on, babe," Nick whined, hips pumping in desperation. "I need you."

*The Gift*

# CHAPTER TWO

"Promise me this one favor first." She swiveled her hips again, teasing the oversensitive head of his cock. Keeping his hands pinned above his head with one hand, she delved her other hand between their bodies to tease her clit. Damn, that felt good. She was so close to coming that she didn't think she would last until she had his agreement. "Consider it my Christmas gift." She released his hands just long enough to wiggle out of her bra and tossed it onto the floor.

"Okay. Dammit. Tell me what you want. I'll do anything. Just sit down on my cock now, before I explode." When he bucked his hips, she ground herself against him. The downy hair around his cock teased her naked lips, and she sighed in bliss as she sank home, his cock stretching her fully. She released his hands, and in one swift motion, he bucked upward and flipped her onto her back.

"How did you do that?" she asked, bewildered, staring up into his smoldering green eyes. "Your cock is still inside me. You didn't even slip out." She writhed under him, her hand grasping his tight ass and pulling him hard against her. "Damn, I love your cock. Have I mentioned that lately?"

He pulled back so only the tip remained inside her. "Only every time I called. And I seem to remember a few naughty text messages that you will need to be punished for." He straightened his arms, pushed his cock in fully, and looked down at her. "You were very bad while I was gone," he warned softly. Sammy knew whatever punishment he meted out would be delightful even while it hurt.

Copying her earlier motion, he captured her hands and pinned them over her head. "Now," he growled teasingly, "tell me what this little favor of yours is." He moved in and out of her with agonizing slowness. She could feel her inner muscles clenching as she neared orgasm, the slippery lips of her pussy sliding along the length of his cock.

She blushed beet red and turned her head aside. Now that she had his agreement, sort of, she hesitated to tell him what she wanted. No, what she needed. To her mortification, he laughed at her.

"Oh-ho," he teased. "So this little favor of yours is of a sexual nature, is it?" He leaned forward to suckle her breast and nibble its pebbly tip. "Damn, you taste good," he murmured. He straightened to look at her again. "Tan lines? This late in November?" He stared at the faint line running low across her belly. "Tanning booth?" he ground out through gritted teeth as he pumped slowly.

"Yes," she whispered in embarrassment. "I had no choice." She turned her head away, another blush coloring her.

"What nasty thing did you do?" he asked sternly, stopping the motion of his hips.

Sammy writhed beneath him. "Nothing," she lied, trying to keep a straight face.

"Tell me," he demanded, pulling out entirely and pausing with the tip of his cock poised at the entrance of her quivering heat. She had tortured him into agreement, and he fully intended to repay the favor until she confessed.

In a rush, she blurted out that she had seen a woman in the mall. A gorgeous blonde with long, shapely legs, a flat stomach, and the most enticing breasts Sammy had ever seen. "I was kind of following her," Sammy confessed, "trying to figure out how to talk to her." She shrugged as if to brush off the event. Nick rewarded her partial confession by easing the tip of his cock back into her.

"And?"

"Well, she went into this tanning place... " Her words trailed off. "And I kind of had to pretend I wanted a tan. You know," she blurted, trying vainly to thrust her hips upward against him. "You know, to have a reason for being there."

"And how precisely does this fit into your little favor?" Nick asked. "The tan is nice." He trailed his tongue alone the line between milky white and light tan skin. He nibbled one nipple before turning his attention to the other. Her pussy gushed wet, and he knew she was thinking something dirty. "What dirty little thoughts are you thinking? You might as well confess right now. I know that naughty little mind of yours."

"I want a woman," she blurted, her pussy gushing arousal once again.

"Do you?" Nick teased. He had often thought that she might be a little bisexual. He had noticed her checking out women, but they had never discussed it before. "Like a maid?" He pretended to be puzzled.

"No." She smacked him lightly on the shoulder and lifted her head to nuzzle the spot. "Don't tease me. It's hard enough to ask as it is." She paused and took a deep breath. "I want to make love to a woman." She blushed again. "You can watch, or help, if you want to," she added in a conciliatory fashion.

Nick started fucking her with long, slow strokes, enjoying the way her pussy quivered around his cock. Damn, she was aroused. This whole idea of a little girl-on-girl action was driving her over the edge. His cock swelled at the thought of watching her sucking on another woman's breasts. He thrust into her hard and stopped moving. When she whimpered in protest, he persisted in his line of questioning. "How do I figure into this?"

"I want you to find a woman for me to sleep with," she whispered, almost begging. "Please." She bucked against him, trying to get him moving again. "Fuck me," she pleaded.

"So, my little sex kitten wants to suck on another woman's breasts, does she?" He asked, knowing his words would arouse her even further.

Sammy nodded, her face flushed with mortification. Sammy's embarrassment surprised Nick. Throughout their relationship, they had indulged in many games and fantasies. Some had been a whole lot of fun and some so disastrous as to be funny. It had been years since Nick had seen her this embarrassed by her desires.

Nick's tongue wreaked havoc with her nipples. "And do you want to lick her pussy? Suck on her soft, wet lips and tongue her sweet clit?" he asked, his words provocative. Sammy groaned and twisted under the dual assault of his words and touch. "Tell me," he demanded.

"Yes," she groaned. "I need to feel a woman's soft body under mine. I need to feel our breasts rubbing together. Oh God, all that soft skin and her hot, wet pussy." Sammy's embarrassment was gone.

Her clenching pussy threatened to crush Nick's cock. He couldn't remember the last time she had been this over the top with desire. Slowly, he pulled out and slammed back into her. With each stroke, Sammy rose up to meet him, her hips bucking and jumping against him. "Please," she begged, unable to form a coherent sentence under the pressures of her mounting desire. "Please. Nick. Fuck me." She felt the first waves of her orgasm piling up, threatening to rush over.

Abruptly he stopped moving. "What do you need?" he asked, merciless in his teasing. He knew how close she was and how much waiting would enhance her orgasm.

"You, I need you. Fuck me. Her voice was husky and broken with desire as she bucked upward, her hips jerking up and slamming against him, pushing him over the edge. "Please."

Unable to hold back any longer, Nick slammed into her, his hips crushing against her, driving his pubic bone into her clit while his cock stroked her pulsing inner walls. Frantic for release, he forgot about teasing and game playing as he pumped into Sammy, his urgent need matching hers. He pulsed and tensed, his testicles pulling up tight and hard.

"Ung. Damn." He panted and groaned, tortured moans ripping from his throat as he gave in to the pressure and spent himself inside her.

"Please," she whispered her voice dry and harsh. She felt herself grow even slicker with a fresh wave of moisture as the first wave of her orgasm crashed over her. Lightning bolts of electricity jerked through her, pinging off her nipples, shivering along her limbs, and lodging in her clit, making her pussy clench and grab at his hardness. Nick's groin ground against hers as he pumped his release, the harsh pounding giving her wave after wave of pleasure. Her legs stiffened, her arms clutched at him, and her lips found his, her mouth swallowing the sounds of his desire. She pumped under him, almost unable to move under the onslaught of her own orgasm.

Spent, Nick dropped down on top of her, panting and shivering in the aftermath of his release. At length he rolled off, taking her into his arms. "Damn," he groaned and nuzzled her hair. "Are you okay? I worry sometimes that I'll hurt you when it's wild like this."

"Mm. Hurt me?" Sammy laughed. "Oh, babe, that was fabulous." She wiggled contentedly against him. "Thanks." Closing her eyes, she drifted toward sleep. "Love you," she mumbled.

"I love you too."

Nick watched Sammy sleeping for as long as he could keep his eyes open. Damn, he loved this woman. His life just wouldn't be complete without her. As he watched, he puzzled about how to grant her request. Sammy didn't ask for much. She was a happy, contented woman, and if she made a request it was only after much thinking and soul-searching. He had to do this for her. The question was how.

♥♥♥

He woke long before she did and had a quick shower before climbing back into bed, lying alongside her to watch her sleep. "Wake up, sleepyhead," Nick's voice teased. "It's morning, and we've got things to do."

"Ugh." She rolled over, trying to ignore him.

"You crack me up," he teased. "They say men fall asleep after sex. Funny it's always you and never me." If it weren't for the brunch date they had with her sister, he would have let her sleep longer. "Into the shower with you." He wrenched off the sheet, landed a playful smack on her ass, and headed for the shower.

"So," he asked through the translucent curtain as Sammy started soaping up. "Just how do you expect me to find a woman?

I mean, how the hell do you ask someone to come home and fuck your wife? A man, sure—it's different with guys. But a woman? Damn." He watched her hands stroking up and down her body, her motions slow and sensual, and although he knew she was baiting him, he couldn't help but become aroused.

Sammy poked her head around the curtain. "Not my problem. You agreed—you figure it out." She stuck her tongue out at him and retreated back into the shower. "What about all those women at work? There was that little redhead at the party last night or maybe that blonde with the luscious tits. You know, the one wearing the hot pink sequined dress. Plus you've mentioned at least a few who seemed to be hitting on you." She fell silent a moment. "Maybe it could be a group thing. You, me, and her." She rinsed and shut the water off. Drawing the curtain aside, she added. "How hard can it be?"

Nick glanced down at the bulge in his pants. How hard could it be? Damned hard!

# CHAPTER THREE

Three weeks later, Nick was stymied. "How hard can it be?" Nick muttered to himself on the drive home from work. How did you even ask such a thing? Besides, none of the girls at work seemed like the right fit. He shook his head in dismay. "Damn, damn, damn." It was already December, and he was no closer to granting her wish than the day he'd started his quest.

He had signed up for several on-line dating sights and done some fishing there. The few nibbles he had were from men or couples, not at all what he was looking for. Many responses were, to say the least, creepy. Very, very creepy. He shared an active and adventurous sex life with Sammy, but nothing they ever did had even come close to some of those suggestions. Geez. Some people were almost too weird to be believed.

## *The Gift*

In a way, he was relieved. He didn't really want to introduce a stranger to their bed, but he was at a loss as to where to look next. He supposed he could hire a professional, but somehow that didn't seem quite right. This needed to be more personal.

On a whim, he decided to approach his old friend Carl about the problem and see if he had any ideas. Nick had met Carl in high school, and they had quickly become friends. They were college roommates, and over the years they had shared everything from an apartment to exam questions, and even, on one or two very memorable occasions, women.

Taking the bull by the horns, he called his old friend to be sure he was home and headed over to Carl's condo for a visit and a little man-to-man talk.

"Damn, I wish I had your kinds of problems." Carl shook his blond head. After only a few seconds of thought, he added, "Gina would do it."

Instantly, a vision of Carl's steady girlfriend popped into Nick's head. Gina was about five foot five and a hundred thirty-five pounds, which made her about the same height as Sammy but a touch thinner. Her breasts were small and perky.

"Jesus." Carl moaned and downed his beer in one swallow. "Can't you see it? Sammy's blonde curls and big tits and

Gina's straight black hair and tiny boobs. What a contrast. Their breasts rubbing together—I would pay money to see that."

"Are you saying you want to fuck my wife?" Nick asked, not sure how he felt about that in spite of having shared women with his friend in the past.

"Hell, yeah, from the first time I laid eyes on her." He grinned roguishly. "When you brought her home that first night, I couldn't decide who I wanted more, you or her." He raked his hands through his short, blond hair, and his hand fell to his lap to cup his cock.

Seeing Carl touch himself made Nick's cock throb at the memory of the times they had loved each other in college. He had a sudden memory of taking Carl's cock in his mouth. He leaned back against the sofa and rubbed a hand across his groin, trying to relieve the pressure building there.

Carl looked at his friend and college lover. "Ever want Gina?"

"Hell, yeah. I'm human, aren't I?" Nick stroked himself through his jeans again.

"Well, technically, that's still up for debate," Carl countered, and they both laughed.

They fell silent a moment, each lost in memories. Carl shifted in his seat, his hand sliding inside his loose pants. Nick watched without comment, mentally drooling at the growing bulge. His own cock twitched in response when Carl pulled his long shaft out and began stroking it. For a moment, Carl toyed with the curly hairs cushioning his balls before he resumed stroking. His hand moved up and down his long, thick cock, and it grew even longer as Nick watched.

"Sammy has the sexiest tits." Carl grinned at Nick. "I would love to tit-fuck her." Nick stroked himself through his jeans before giving up the fight and unzipping and pulling his cock out. It had been years since they masturbated together. At one time it had been a favorite pastime. Jerking off, watching each other, and talking about the people they would love to fuck.

As if reading Nick's mind, Carl said, "Remember Missy Algonquin? Now there was a fuckable ass."

Nick laughed. "Tighter than any other ass I've fucked, except yours."

"You tapped that?" Carl pumped faster, his hips squirming in the chair. "I never worked up the nerve to try." He sighed. "I was such a wimp in college. No balls at all."

"Oh, yeah, she was good."

"Gina loves it up the ass," Carl gloated in an abrupt conversation shift that was typical for him. "Sammy?"

"She's a little gun shy yet. But I'm working on it." His cock twitched at the thought of being buried deep inside his wife's tight ass while she devoured another woman's pussy. "Okay, Gina it is," Nick declared, abruptly returning the discussion to his problem. He squeezed gently on the tip of his cock to slow his escalation. Just the image of his wife with Gina was enough to set him off.

"One condition," Carl panted, his motions becoming frantic.

"Hngph," Nick grunted.

Carl was on his feet in a second, his pants kicked aside as he moved to stand in front of Nick, his erection straining and throbbing in front of him. "I get to fuck Sammy, too."

Nick released his grip on his cock and leaned forward to lick Carl's length, loving the salty taste of his precum. "Can't guarantee that," he choked out, taking Carl into his mouth.

Carl pulled back. "You gotta try, man." Nick leaned in, trying to draw Carl back into his mouth. "Promise you'll try." Nick grunted his agreement, and Carl grabbed him by the hair and rammed his cock into Nick's mouth.

Carl was the only man Nick had ever had sex with, and it had been years since he sucked him off, but some things were never forgotten. Nick swallowed hard, eased his breathing, and greedily engulfed his best friend. His tongue flicked over Carl's head, and Nick wrapped one hand around the base and cupped Carl's balls with the other, rolling them between his fingers.

Carl groaned and pumped hard. "Suck me, man. Hard." Nick obliged and pumped with his hand and his mouth. Carl's cock was swelling in his mouth, and Nick knew his friend was close. Without slowing his strokes, Nick used his tongue to push Carl's length against the roof of his mouth. He flattened his tongue and stroked it up and down Carl's cock without releasing the suction.

"Ahh." Carl jerked against Nick's tongue. He was so close to exploding it felt like his balls were going to come out through the head of his cock. Suddenly he was there, one deep, massive shiver from nuts to tip. His testicles drew up tight, his shaft swelled, and he knew he was finished. "Damn." He thrust his hips three times, pulled out, and exploded in Nick's hand.

Carl dropped to his knees to recover from the residual weakness of his release. "Damn, nobody ever sucked me off like you," he breathed. Still kneeling, he grabbed the waistband of Nick's jeans and tugged. Nick lifted his hips, his stiff cock waving in the air as Carl disposed of the denim. "How do you want it?" Carl offered, even though he already knew the answer.

"Chair," Nick grunted. Carl suppressed a smile. That was what he loved about Nick—he was consistent. Crawling toward the chair, he waggled his ass back at his friend and purred, "Come get me." Digging in a coffee table drawer, he extracted a silver pouch and threw it at Nick before kneeling on the chair. "Safety first," he teased, knowing the delay would drive Nick wild.

Nick's fingers fumbled so much; it took three tries to open the package. It might have helped if Carl hadn't been kneeling on the arms of the chair, legs spread, his arms braced on the chair back, his ass in the air, waiting. Practice makes perfect, and Nick had the condom on in seconds but stood stroking himself, staring at the bounty laid out before him. Damn, he had missed this.

"Hold tight, lover," he growled, rubbing himself along the crease of Carl's ass. He moistened himself with a bit of saliva, placed the tip at the entrance to Carl's puckered hole, and paused. "You ready?" The question wasn't even a courtesy. Frankly, he didn't care if Carl was ready or not. He was. Even before he finished asking, he was driving himself in.

Carl pushed back against him. Nick loved the way he slid in so fully, so quickly. Nick knew Carl would love the feeling of having his ass filled after so long, and that it would have Carl hard again in no time. It had always been a game for them to see who could make the other lose control the fastest.

"I'm gonna fuck your wife, man," Carl goaded and laughed when Nick swore and thrust harder.

"And I'm gonna fuck your girlfriend's ass while I watch her suck my wife's pussy. I'm gonna fuck her hard, just like I'm doing to you." He slammed harder. What the hell had Sammy gotten him into? This was going to end up a foursome, he just knew it. And, dammit all to hell, he wanted it. Leaning back, he slapped Carl on the ass before slamming back in.

Reaching around, Nick grabbed hold of Carl's cock and pumped it back to life. "Come on, man," he groaned. Driving in and out as hard as he could without releasing that gorgeous erection, he took his friend hard and fast, just the way they both liked it. He pounded into him again and again until the pressure became too much to bear and he knew he was going to finish faster than he wanted to.

Carl reveled in the pounding he was taking, his ass stretched and abused while Nick fucked him. It was just like the good old days, and he pumped his hips forward and back, driving Nick's cock deeper into him, pumping into Nick's hand. Without warning, Nick's cock began to twitch in Carl's ass, and Carl knew his friend was losing the battle to delay his orgasm. When Nick slammed into him with a grunt, it tipped Carl over the edge, and he exploded into Nick's hand once more.

Satiated, they stayed there for a few moments. Nick slumped against Carl's back, reveling in the renewal of the part of their relationship that had been lost when Nick found Sammy. "Damn, I missed you." Nick placed a kiss on Carl's shoulder and pulled his spent member out. He wrapped the condom in a tissue and tossed it into the wastebasket. He grabbed a shirt from the basket of clean laundry sitting on the floor and began to wipe up with it.

Carl dropped to the chair. "Shit." He jumped up, grabbing the shirt from Nick. "There's cum all over my brand new chair."

"Just like old times." Nick laughed. "We didn't own one stick of furniture that didn't have splooge all over it." They laughed together and sat side by side on the couch, thighs just touching.

"So," Carl asked when they had regained their breath. "How do we do this thing?" They settled back, hands entwined, and began planning the seduction of Sammy.

***The Gift***

# CHAPTER FOUR

"Carl hasn't been over for months. You usually just go to his place. Why the sudden change of routine?" Sammy asked, pulling her sweater off over her head and tossing it into the hamper in the corner of their bedroom.

Nick shrugged and studied her, enjoying the way her breasts looked in her red lace bra. "No idea. But when we had beers last week, we decided it was a good idea. I guess it's just the holiday season. It makes me want to keep in touch with old friends. Maybe it's the Christmas spirit." He stepped up behind her, wrapping his arms loosely around her waist. "We've been friends for so long, we thought it might be nice if you and Gina were friends too."

"I can't wait to meet her." Sammy loved meeting new people and entertaining.

"Yeah." Nick moved closer to Sammy and cupped her breasts in his hands. "She's cute. She's got the hottest tits." He ground his erection against his wife's ass, and she pivoted in his arms to face him.

"Did you ever do her?" she asked, knowing part of his history with Carl and feeling more intrigued than jealous.

"No, they got together after I found you and moved out." He nibbled Sammy's ear. "I've known her for a while. She's hot. Her boobs are so perky, and her nipples stick out all the time. Carl says she never wears panties. Just like you." He playfully slapped her ass. "But don't you be staring at her nipples all night. I don't think she's bi." He stifled a smile.

Damn right she's bi, he thought, and Gina was fully into the plan to seduce the eager Sammy. They had agreed to tell Sammy Gina might not be bi, just in case the two women didn't hit it off. If Gina wasn't moved by Sammy, it would be no harm, no foul. Although judging by Carl's stories about his girlfriend, there would be no problem with her being attracted to Sammy. Carl maintained that Gina had a sex drive as high as Sammy's and that she was familiar with Sapphic love.

Unable to stop himself, Nick dropped to his knees and began mouthing Sammy's pert nipples through the lace of her bra. Just thinking of her making love to another woman made him rock-hard. He clutched her ass in his hands and rubbed his cock against her thigh. Even through his jeans, it felt good. Sammy clutched his head and held him to her breast.

"Oh, yeah, suck on my nipple. That feels so good. Love me." She groaned and pushed her breasts against him. "Touch me," she demanded, pushing his hands down toward her aching pussy.

"Tsk, tsk," he scolded, not releasing his hold on her nipple. His hand slid under her skirt and up her thigh. "Holy hell, you're dripping wet," he groaned, rubbing small circles with the flat of his hand against her slippery folds. "You went to work without panties again." He nuzzled her belly. "Naughty girl." He flipped her skirt up, pressing his hands against the insides of her thighs, telling her without words to spread her legs wider.

Obedient to his silent demands, Sammy spread her legs wide, then wider, opening herself to his touch. His breath was hot on her belly. Her skin tingled, and her pussy throbbed and clenched. "Lick me," she demanded.

Nick moved back a little. "Silence," he ordered. "Not one word." He flicked his thumb against her clit. "Not a sound." He flicked again, harder. "And don't move a muscle. You know the rules," he warned his voice husky and dangerous. "One wiggle, one sound, and I'm finished down here, and you'll get your ass spanked." He looked up at her. She gave the tiniest nod of acquiescence, not daring to move more than necessary. "Good girl," he praised, leaning in to blow on her hot folds.

His breath felt like cold fire against her, and Sammy felt a ripple of arousal race through her. She twitched but didn't move. Sometimes she deliberately moved, driving him to follow up on his threat and spank her. Today, she needed an orgasm, fast, so she remained motionless.

Nick's tongue made a broad, flat stroke against her, and her thighs clenched. He licked again, one finger toying with her ass. Her belly quivered, and she sucked in a breath. Her pussy clenched. She felt a little drop of moisture seep out. Nick flicked his tongue back and forth over her lips, carefully avoiding her distended clit, sliding one finger into her heat.

"You are very wet, Naughty Girl." He licked again, his finger pushing against her puckered hole.

His words and actions were almost her undoing. Her legs quivered, she shivered from head to toe and she gasped and swallowed her cry of delight. Nick wiggled his finger in her ass and slid another one into her pussy. "Come on girl, give it to me. Give me your pleasure. Come for me while I finger your cunt. Come on, Sammy, you know you love it."

Biting her lip to keep from screaming, she stared down at him. Damn, she loved him. Their eyes met, and she could see his love shining there along with his arousal. She shivered again but dared not move. She knew if she did he would deny her the pleasure she so desperately needed. Her core pulsed and clenched, twitching against his fingers as her arousal grew.

"Touch your breasts," he ordered, his breath coming in harsh gasps. "Play with those sweet nipples. Pinch them hard." Helpless to deny him, and not really wanting to anyway, she cupped a breast in each hand, framing her nipples with her fingers. She loved how they pebbled under her touch. She tweaked them hard. Then harder.

Feeling her pussy spasm against his hand, Nick knew she was on the edge. "Now," he decreed. That one word was both a command and permission. Pinching and twisting her nipples, she thrust her pussy against his questing fingers, shuddered hugely, and came. Hot moisture gushed over Nick's fingers, drenching his hand. He smiled up at Sammy and leaned in to taste her release.

Weak-kneed, Sammy clutched Nick's shoulders to stay upright. He always knew exactly what she needed. Slow and tender, fast and hard. He even knew when she needed to surrender completely to his command, like now. Her job was stressful, some days more than others. She had spent the entire day on the edge of kicking someone's ass or firing someone for a minor offense. It had taken every ounce of willpower she possessed to keep her cool and not come unglued. Knowing Nick was at home to vent with was the only thing that kept her in check. When he took command, it allowed her to step back, give in, and surrender control, and in doing so unwind and regroup.

Regaining her equilibrium in spite of his questing tongue, she released his shoulders and stroked his head. Twitching against his lips, she reveled in the soft feel of his mouth on her arousal. He was good at this, she thought. "Come to the bed," she urged, pulling at his arm in a vain attempt to get him to stand.

"No time." Reluctantly, he withdrew from between her legs. "They'll be here right away."

"Just one more orgasm," she pleaded, even though she knew it was hopeless. There just wasn't enough time, and part of their game demanded that she follow his dictates and wait for her next release.

Nick laughed and slapped her ass lightly. "Get your sweet ass in the shower, or I won't let you come again tonight."

# CHAPTER FIVE

When Sammy emerged from the shower, it was to find an outfit she had never seen before displayed on the bed. She could hear voices coming from downstairs and knew she was running behind. Thank goodness everything was ready for dinner. Nick would have served their guests drinks already. Laughter bubbled up the stairs, and Sammy raced to get dressed.

A quick application of body lotion and a squirt of Nick's favorite perfume came first. Then she slipped into the lacy bra and panty set. Emerald green trimmed with black lace, they looked exquisite against her new tan. She turned around to study herself in the mirror. The lacy boy-briefs cuddled her ass, and she took a moment to admire and stroke them before slipping into the skirt and silk top. The skirt was some kind of slippery, black material, the top emerald silk. Smoothing them against her curves, she noticed the skirt was shorter than she usually wore and the blouse cut quite low.

Staring at herself in the mirror, she worried a bit about meeting Carl's girlfriend for the first time. She wanted to make a good impression. Nick and Carl had been friends for years, and she knew Nick had missed their closeness. She didn't want to interfere with their friendship by offending Gina. Worried, she slipped into the heels Nick had set out for her and moved away from the mirror.

There was a slip of paper taped to the bedroom door. *Stop second-guessing yourself*, the note advised in Nick's handwriting. *You look stunning. Now get your ass downstairs and join us.* He'd signed the note with a panting happy face. She laughed and opened the door. *Well, here goes nothing*, she thought as she headed down the stairs.

She found them in the kitchen. Nick and Carl stood shoulder to shoulder against the counter and somehow managed to look strangely intimate. None of them noticed Sammy at first, and she took a moment to study Gina, who sat on the island counter facing the men, swinging her feet.

*Holy hell, she's hot*, was Sammy's first thought, staring at the dark-haired woman sitting on her counter. Her hair was deep brown, almost black, and fell poker-straight to well past her shoulders. It shone under the bright lights of the kitchen. She had a sweet, turned-up nose and pale creamy skin.

Gina was average in height and thin but not too skinny. She was wearing a scoop-neck blouse, and Sammy found her eyes drawn to Gina's breasts and the places where her hard nipples poked against her shirt. She's not wearing a bra, and damn, Nick was right, she does have nice tits. A very, very short skirt covered only the tops of Gina's slender legs—legs Sammy felt a sudden urge to touch. She was wearing black stilettos with tiny jewels glittering on the heels, and Sammy could just see the tops of her stockings and garters. Too bad Nick had said she wasn't bi. Just looking at her was making Sammy all hot and fluttery in the belly.

Gina noticed Sammy the second she paused in the kitchen doorway. She chose not to acknowledge the other woman immediately; instead, Gina took sneaking glances at her and let Sammy look her fill.

Gina's first sexual encounter had been with another woman, and since that first glorious occasion, she had enjoyed both women and men equally. Six months ago, she had fallen in love with Carl and hadn't touched a woman since. She hadn't really wanted to. Sure, she had enjoyed looking, but the urge to touch and play had been absent. Until now. As she sat watching Sammy staring greedily at her, Gina was struck by the sudden thought that she could love this woman.

*The Gift*

Sammy was about five six with generous curves. Sexy curves, Gina thought. She had beautiful blue eyes and nice, C-cup breasts. Gina's fingers itched to trace every curve of that sweet body until she had memorized every inch. Her short skirt revealed lean, toned, sexy legs, and her low-cut blouse showed off her cleavage, making Gina's mouth water. Hot damn, I'm going to enjoy this. She banked a sudden desire to make love to Sammy and to hold her tight and keep her close.

Knowing the men were watching the women size each other up without letting on, Gina flashed them a quick look that said she was definitely in. She was going to seduce Sammy, and it might not happen in the future as originally planned. It might be right here, right now. She could hardly wait to kiss these pert, pink lips.

"Babe." Nick moved to stand beside his wife. "You remember Carl." At her nod he added, "This is his girlfriend, Gina. Gina, this is my wife, Sammy."

Gina hopped off the counter and landed lightly on her stiletto heels. Her breasts bounced, nearly popping out of her shirt. Sammy nearly choked at the rush of desire that swamped her from the quick peek at those tawny nipples. Moving by rote, she offered her hand. "Hi. It's nice to meet you." Their fingers touched and time slowed. Gina's hand was soft and feminine, her fingers long and well-manicured. Her gentle touch and firm shake left Sammy's entire arm tingling, her mouth dry, her nipples hard.

To Sammy's surprise, Gina pulled her into her arms and hugged her close. It was a quick hug, but long enough to feel the hard peaks of Gina's nipples pressing against her own. Sammy felt weak-kneed with longing and felt herself moisten with desire. Loath to let Gina's hot body move away for fear of never touching it again, Sammy dropped her arm around Gina's waist and walked with her back to the counter.

Sammy let Gina steer her toward the far side of the island. Side by side, they leaned against it, facing Nick and Carl. Following Gina's lead, Sammy leaned over, resting on one elbow, her breasts on the counter, her other arm still around Gina. Gina's arm snaked around Sammy's waist, and her fingers stroked softly at Sammy's side.

Sammy cast Gina a quick look of confusion. Gina smiled widely and winked. She leaned toward Sammy and, with her breath tickling Sammy's ear, whispered, "Those two are just about the nicest pieces of fine I've ever seen. Aren't they?" For a moment, Sammy thought she felt Gina nuzzle her hair before she pulled back to stare at the men, her chin cupped in her hand.

Nothing ventured, nothing gained, Sammy thought and leaned toward Gina to whisper, "Damned kissable, the pair of them." She flicked her tongue out, barely brushing Gina's ear. Her touch was light enough it could be considered an accident, but firm enough Gina might take it as a come on.

"They're so hot," Gina whispered back. Her hand slipped lower, coming to rest on the top of Sammy's ass.

Sammy tensed, stilled, and then relaxed against Gina's hand. "Kissable," she agreed with a giggle. Surely her arm had just slipped. Gina wasn't touching Sammy's ass on purpose, was she?

"No, delectable," Gina declared, pushing her breast against Sammy's.

This time, Sammy had no doubt Gina's actions were deliberate, and she pressed back. "Lickable," she whispered, her lips brushing Gina's ear.

"Hey, what are you two whispering about over there?" Nick demanded, breaking off his conversation with Carl.

Gina and Sammy looked at each other. "Fuckable," Gina whispered, and they broke out laughing. Sammy dropped her hand to brush lightly against Gina's ass and turned slightly toward her. Damn, Sammy thought, I am completely horny already. She's barely touched me and I'm dripping wet. My pussy feels like it's on fire.

Gina turned into the half-embrace and slipped both hands around Sammy's waist. Sammy found her arms slipping around Gina's neck. Before Sammy realized what was happening, Gina was leaning into her, her lips parted and moist. She's going to kiss me, Sammy thought in a moment of panic. Gina inched closer, and Sammy realized with sudden clarity that she wanted this. She wanted to taste those soft lips. Here. Now. In front of Nick and Carl. She didn't care who was watching. An audience was just going to make this hotter by fueling her exhibitionist tendencies.

"Yes," she breathed, closing the distance. She pressed her lips softly to Gina's, marveling at how different they were from Nick's. They were smaller, softer, sweeter, and very enticing. They kissed for a moment before Gina's tongue darted out to touch Sammy's lips. She sucked in a startled breath and opened her mouth to allow access. "Oh," she breathed against Gina's lips, tingles of arousal darting through her to lodge in her femininity, making her moist and hot.

Gina's lips were soft and sweet to start, but when Sammy started pressing back, pressing harder against her, Gina increased the pressure and let her hands wander over the deep curve of Sammy's waist, up her side and back down, caressing, teasing.

Sammy writhed under Gina's touch, forgetting for the moment that they had an audience. It felt so good to be pressed against Gina's soft curves. Gina's nipples were like rocks against Sammy, and she felt her own harden in response to their pressure. Gina cradled Sammy's head in one hand and trailed her fingers up Sammy's left arm, leaving tingles in her wake, teasing and touching, moving slowly but undeniably toward the neckline of Sammy's shirt. Oh yes, please touch me. Come on, Gina, I need to feel your hands on my breasts. Sammy's mind careened out of control as her body came to life under Gina's attentions.

Gina trailed her fingers along the inner edge of Sammy's shirt and smiled against her mouth when Sammy shivered under that light touch. She traced the curve of the neckline down and up the other side, first with one finger, then with two, then three. Sammy panted against her mouth. "Do you like that?" Gina whispered her voice low and moist against Sammy's ear and neck.

Sammy gasped, but said nothing, so Gina traced the curve of her breast with her lips. "Oh," Sammy cried, powerless to contain the sound of her arousal. Sammy's nipples hardened in response to the kiss, and she grew damp with arousal. She breathed deeply, inhaling the musk of Gina's perfume and the sweet scent of her arousal. Her nostrils flared as she realized Gina was sharing her arousal. Fortifying herself, unable to shake the fear of rejection, Sammy moved her mouth to Gina's neck, placing soft nuzzling kisses there, tasting the delicate flavor of her skin.

Gina's breathing turned thready, and Sammy pressed her pursuit, tasting the hollow at the base of Gina's throat, feeling the pulse thumping there before moving lower. She pushed aside the soft linen of Gina's shirt, delving with her lips and tongue until she found the gently curving slope of Gina's breast. With trembling hands, Sammy eased aside the linen, making room for her questing mouth.

She followed that curve down and teased the underside of Gina's breast, the soft responsive flesh fueling her own arousal, driving her to new heights. She licked the gentle up-slope and felt Gina's hard nipple tickle her nose. Moving in slow circles, she spiraled her way toward the nipple, tasting, loving, and teasing. Sammy felt the first pebbling of Gina's areola under her tongue and swallowed hard, breathed deep, and flicked her tongue over the nipple.

Yes, she thought, this is what I've been waiting for. With a rush of silent pleasure and anticipation, she took Gina's nipple into her mouth and sucked gently on it, feeling her own nipple twitch and harden in response, almost as if a mouth were caressing her as well. Gina's nipple pebbled even harder at the touch of Sammy's mouth, and they sighed in unison. Without releasing her hold, Sammy smiled up at Gina, her eyes betraying her own arousal.

Gina loved the way Sammy cupped Gina's breasts in her hands and lavished attention on one, then the other. Gina wiggled under the gentle touch. Sammy's touches were incredibly arousing, in spite of being shy and tentative, but from the rapid beating of Sammy's heart and the rushed sounds of her breathing, Gina knew her new friend was aroused. That boded well for both of them. There was a sweet thrill to breaking in a virgin like this. She let her own hands drift higher, caressing Sammy through her blouse, exploring the curve of her waist and cupping one breast, delighting in the weight of it in her hand.

It had been a long time since Gina had made love to another woman, and she had almost forgotten the pure pleasure of mimicking her lover's motions and using the echoed touches to fuel her own desire. It was sweet heaven, made even sweeter by the men who stood there staring in rapt attention at the erotic scene unfolding before them.

Gina fondly remembered her initiation into Sapphic love. It had been very private and special. She worried that Sammy might become embarrassed when she realized how public their loving was. After several agonizing moments of self-doubt, Gina decided to indulge herself a little before bringing their touching to a gentle halt. As much as they were all enjoying this, she knew that in the end it would be better for waiting.

Sammy realized Gina was copying her motions and strokes. She found it very erotic and exciting, and reveled in the rush of power it gave her to learn she was leading the way, setting the pace. She flicked her thumbs over Gina's nipples and writhed when Gina mimicked the touch. She leaned in to kiss

Gina's neck, titling her head to the side to allow Gina's mouth access to her own neck.

Sweet, moist heat settled at the juncture of Sammy's thighs as she loved and was loved in return. She pinched Gina's nipples lightly, her sex gushing when Gina pinched back. She increased the pressure, not enough to hurt, just enough to tease and entice. Her knees went weak at the duplicate pressure on her own nipples.

Oh, this feels so good. When Gina whispered it was fabulous, Sammy realized that she had spoken aloud. Briefly, she stilled her motions, embarrassed, but Gina's next words comforted Sammy. "Don't be embarrassed. You are so beautiful." Gina's voice was low and soft. "You feel lovely, and you make me feel so nice." She eased her hands lower, settling them on Sammy's hips. "I want this, more than anything," she murmured softly. "But not here. I want you on a bed where I can love you properly."

Slowly, her words penetrated the fog of arousal in Sammy's head, and she flushed with embarrassment and her hands fell motionless to her side. "Don't worry. It's only you and I here." She tipped her head toward the men. "And them, and look at how hard they are."

Sammy glanced at the men and looked away almost instantly. In that brief glance, she could see they were indeed fully aroused. They stood there, shoulders touching, each with an impressive bulge in his pants. A shiver raced through her. They were enticed by watching her with Gina. A rush of arousal swamped her, threatening to buckle her knees. Oh my! She glanced back at them, and Nick gave her a huge grin.

The bastard! He had planned this all along. And she had nobody to blame but herself. She had asked for this. She smiled hugely and laughed aloud. Damned if she didn't love him even more for this.

"Well, now the entertainment is finished," she quipped, "shall we eat?" The double entendre hit her, and she gave a chagrined laugh. "Don't say it," she warned, her hand tangling with Gina's. "I meant food."

# CHAPTER SIX

Nick had watched in shock as Gina and Sammy began kissing. He wasn't surprised that Sammy found Gina attractive, but it did shock him that she'd started necking with a woman she had known only minutes, and dammit, didn't it make him rock hard? Beside him, he could hear Carl's breathing accelerate and knew his friend was as aroused as he was. He was torn. Should they stay and watch the erotica unfold, or should they make a discreet exit and allow the girls some privacy?

He found himself moving reluctantly away. This was for Sammy, not for him. Yet.

The feel of Carl's hand on his arm stopped his creeping motion. "Wait," Carl whispered, almost too low to hear. "Gina loves an audience. Stay until one of them tells us to leave." Nick stared in shock at Carl. "You said she was willing to share with you," Carl mouthed. "This is sharing too."

Since he couldn't find a rational way to dispute Carl's assertion, Nick leaned back against the counter and turned his attention back to the drama unfolding in front of them. He felt Carl's arm slide around his waist, his fingers sneaking into the waistband of Nick's jeans. He slanted his friend a questioning look. Carl knew Sammy was unaware of the full extent of the history between the two men. Carl flashed him an unapologetic, roguish grin and shrugged.

Nick glanced down to discover his own erection was matched by Carl's, and a thrill ran through him, hardening him even further. Damn, it would be nice to touch each other while the women played together. Just thinking about it made him restless and excited. Carl chuckled in his ear and wiggled his hand further down Nick's waistband. Nick shifted to allow better access and said a quick thank you that he wasn't wearing a belt and had on very loose pants.

Carl's hand was warm on his ass, and Nick squirmed when he gripped it tight, his large hand spanning one cheek, his nails pressing deep into the firm flesh. Carl squeezed and tormented him, and Nick throbbed in response. That was how it had always been with Carl. Hard, fast, and rough. The contrast between the rough treatment behind him and the beautiful, soft loving in front of him was wildly arousing, and Nick knew that if this double stimulation continued much longer he was in danger of losing control, dropping to his knees, and taking Carl's cock into his mouth. Only the thought that Sammy didn't yet know about his past kept him in check.

Both Nick and Carl were torn between disappointment and relief when their ladies pulled apart. It would have been so good to continue their own games while watching the girls. But they knew the mind was the body's biggest sexual organ, and the anticipation would only heighten the pleasure for all of them.

♥♥♥

The four of them sat around the dining table, sipping wine. Dinner had been fabulous in spite of the delay in eating. Even after the girls had finally stepped apart to finish the meal preparation, it had taken a long time to get the food ready. Progress had been hampered by pauses for kissing and touching, and in one very memorable occasion, a break for the ladies to pull up their shirts and rub their naked breasts together.

They were clearing the table after dinner when Gina suddenly said, "Do you have any Pimm's? I have such a craving for Pimm's." It took only minutes to dispatch the men to find a bottle of the imported gin. As they headed out the door she called, "Don't forget the lemonade, strawberries, oranges and mint leaves."

"Okay," Gina confessed to Sammy. "I do love Pimm's, but I don't really want any right now." She smiled sensually. "I just wanted them gone for a while so we could be alone." Moving to the couch with their wine, Sammy and Gina sat side by side, their thighs brushing each other. They talked quietly for a few minutes, admiring the Christmas tree and discussing their plans for the rapidly approaching holiday.

When Gina's fingers began slowly stroking her thigh, Sammy blurted out that she had never done this before. "Don't worry, honey," Gina reassured her. "We won't do anything you don't want. But I really, really need to kiss you." She leaned forward, took Sammy's glass, and set it on the table. Pivoting in her seat, she took Sammy's hands in her own and caressed her fingers lightly.

For several long moments they sat and stared into each other's eyes before Sammy worked up the nerve to lean toward Gina. That one small motion was all it took. She leaned in slightly and Gina swooped forward, her hands cupping Sammy's shoulders, her lips pressing against Sammy's. "You taste so good," she murmured, flicking her tongue across Sammy's lips.

Sammy groaned deep in her throat and pulled back. Pivoting on the seat, she turned to get better access to Gina's body. She needed to touch her. She needed to feel those perky breasts in her hands and mouth again, now.

She cupped one breast in her hand and leaned down to kiss the valley exposed by the deep curve of Gina's shirt. She kissed and nuzzled, her mouth moving, tasting and learning, her hips gyrating and pivoting in need. She was frantic with urgency and quickly stripped Gina's loose top off over her head.

She paused a moment to look at Gina's breasts. Small and compact, they had a delightful curve and rock-hard, dark brown nipples. They were the most enticing and erotic sight she had seen in a while. Sammy felt her own nipples harden in response and heat rushed to her groin when she leaned in and began to devour Gina's small breasts.

Each kiss, each caress was like touching herself. Everything she did to Gina echoed in her own body. It was electric. She nuzzled those sweet nipples, moving back and forth between them. Teasing. Sucking. Loving. She flicked them with her tongue, delighted when Gina trembled and bucked under her touches.

Sammy's couldn't believe the contrast in feeling between loving Gina's soft body and loving Nick's rock-hard one. Both were incredible, but this was nice. It was gentle, soft and slow. Moving back, she slipped her own shirt off.

"Oh," Gina moaned, "so pretty." She reached over and cupped Sammy's breasts in her hands. "That green color is perfect for your skin tone," she whispered, leaning in to trace the upper edges of the bra with her tongue. She licked and kissed every inch of exposed breast before slowly releasing the clasp, sliding her hands under the lace and cupping Sammy's breasts. "Your nipples are so hard," she murmured, teasing them with her thumbs.

Sammy writhed under Gina's touch. She wanted more. As if reading her mind, Gina pushed Sammy backward gently, encouraging her to stretch out on the couch. She toyed with Sammy's breasts for a moment before coming to lie with her. She pressed one leg between Sammy's, and kneeling slightly, one hand on either side of Sammy's head, slowly lowered herself until the tips of her breasts lightly brushed against Sammy's larger ones. She moved slowly, her body making small circles, her hard peaks tracing across Sammy's chest. Soft skin against soft skin, Gina's nipples left trails of fire behind, making Sammy writhe when their nipples brushed together.

Gina lowered herself closer, their breasts pushing together, and began kissing Sammy. Their lips melded, their tongues tangling together. Supporting her weight on one elbow,

Gina let her left hand wander, stroking up and down Sammy's side, exploring and teasing.

Sammy reached up, cupped Gina's head in her hands, pulled her close, and kissed her deeply. She trailed her lips across Gina's soft cheek and downward, seeking the pleasure of her nipple. Arousal swamped her as she suckled the eraser-hard nipple while exploring her body with one hand. She teased and sucked hard, then retreated to the softest touch, loving Gina the way she wanted to be loved herself. Gina wiggled and writhed on top of her, her thigh rubbing lightly against the moist heat of Sammy's arousal, rousing them both further.

Sammy twisted under Gina, and Gina increased the pressure of her thigh, moaning softly as the thin fabric of Sammy's panties grew even wetter. Sammy jerked against her leg, then began to move in slow motion, rubbing her pussy against Gina's leg.

Sammy pumped her hips up and down, rubbing then grinding herself against Gina's thigh, each stroke tantalizing and bringing her closer to her peak. She writhed and wiggled, her breath coming in staccato bursts, her motions becoming increasingly frantic as she edged toward the precipice. Deep in her mind, she registered the fact that it might be the quickest orgasm she'd ever had. Closer to the surface, she didn't care. The only thought in her head was the need for satisfaction. She hadn't experienced arousal like this in a long time.

She grew moist, then wet, her panties edging higher and higher, cupping her tightly, pulling against her clit as her moisture coated Gina's leg. She cupped Gina's breasts in her hands and arched her back to take one nipple in her mouth as she stroked and rode Gina's lean, muscled thigh. Gina tugged on Sammy's thigh, drawing it upward to push against her pussy.

"Oh, you are so wet," Sammy cried as Gina's hot, wet pussy ground against Sammy's leg. Sammy copied Gina's motions stroke for stoke. Sammy felt her arousal peaking and knew her orgasm was imminent. Shudders of delight wracked her body, lodging in her cunt, and she pumped harder, rubbing desperately.

"Yes," Gina cried into Sammy's mouth. Her pace became frantic as her orgasm swamped her. She bucked and moaned, her motions never slowing.

Sammy felt a hot gush of moisture against her thigh. The feeling of Gina's release sent her into hers. "Gina, oh..." She panted, grinding against Gina's thigh until she exploded in a ball of heat and sensation.

Gina dropped her weight a little, but not enough to squish Sammy. "Oh," she breathed, "that was lovely."

Still riding her pleasure high, Sammy laughed. "Oh, Gina, you have no idea." She kissed her soundly on the lips. They kissed softly for a few moments, their hands searching unexplored territory, their lips tasting and loving. At length she added, "That was fabulous. So different from a man, so different from Nick, but so nice." She sighed.

Gina rose to her feet gracefully and reached out for Sammy's hand to pull her to her feet. They took a moment to hug and taste each other once more before moving toward the bathroom to clean up. They cuddled and whispered about all the things they wanted to try with each other next time, but for now, the waiting just added to the anticipation. By the time the men arrived back home with the fruits of their search, the girls were seated on the floor in front of the coffee table wrapping Christmas gifts.

Nick and Carl shared a quick, questioning glance. What the hell was going on? They had been sure that the girls were into one another and that they would be in bed together when the men got back. Nick was sure he could smell sex. Its distinctive tang tugged at his senses, fueling the erection he still had from thinking about Sammy and Gina together. But they weren't in bed. Instead they sat beside each other, neat and tidy and giggling about something.

Nick cast a sharp glance at his wife. She looked at him and looked away. Oh-ho, he thought, that was her guilty look. She only had that twisted smile and that gleam in her eye when she had done or was thinking about something naughty. So, they had "entertained" themselves, but for some reason they were keeping it a secret. Interesting.

# CHAPTER SEVEN

Later that night, Nick and Sammy lie side by side in bed talking. Sammy looked him in the eye and knew he was going to demand a full account of her time with Gina. Damn, he'll want details. She felt her pussy spasm in anticipation of sharing them. *Is it wrong that I love talking dirty with him?*

"Okay, my little sex kitten, spill the beans," Nick demanded, rolling to rest slightly on top of her.

"Nope." She loved this part of the game. She loved resisting him, even though they both knew she would give in eventually. It made her so hot when he called her a sex kitten. It made her feel sexy and desirable.

Moving slowly, he clasped her wrists together and pinned them over her head. "I said spill the beans," he growled menacingly. Damn, she loved the way his body pressed hers into the mattress. It made her feel so small and helpless. He thrust his stiffening cock against her belly and repeated himself. Feigning reluctance, she turned her head away and tried to wiggle free of his grasp. "Spill it. Tell me what you girls were up to while Carl and I were off on your boondoggle."

"Nothing," she lied, without even trying to sound convincing. "We just wrapped some gifts and had a glass of wine."

He held her chin in his hand and pressed down threateningly. "Tell. Me. What. You. Did." He bit out each word individually. Sammy shivered with delight; she loved when he pretended to be all tough and dominating. She had her submissive side, and this thrilled her to bits. It was difficult not to wiggle under him and press her pussy against his leg. She shook her head from side to side, trying to dislodge his hand. "Tell me, you naughty girl."

"Really, we just wrapped gifts." Sammy bit back a smile. She knew what was coming next, and Nick didn't disappoint her.

"You are such a lying bitch," he growled, jerking her to her feet and pulling her over his knee. "Now, tell me what you were doing while I was gone. I saw that smug look on your face when we got back." He lifted her nightgown, exposing her naked ass and stroking it menacingly. "Last warning."

"Nothing." Sammy wiggled on his lap, hoping it looked like she was worried rather than anticipating what was coming. She felt her ass cool as he raised his hand warningly. She tensed slightly, knowing this was going to hurt so good. His hand came down with a quick, hard smack.

"Sammy," he warned, raising his hand again.

She writhed on his lap. *Not yet, Nick. I'm feeling naughty tonight, and I need a good spanking.* She braced herself for the next blow. His hand came down again and again, smacking her soundly, making her writhe in exquisite agony. Her ass grew hotter, her pussy wetter. Her nipples throbbed and begged to be sucked. Six, seven—she counted the blows mentally, noting Nick was careful never to hit the same place twice or hit too hard. Eight, nine. She waited, anticipating. And waited.

"Tell me," he demanded again, his hand coming down one more time.

"Okay, okay," she pleaded, almost managing to sound like she meant it. "I touched her." It was an effort, but she managed to make it sound like she was embarrassed or regretted her actions. It was all part of the game, and she loved it.

"Where did you touch her?" Nick raised his hand warningly.

"I touched her breasts and she touched mine," Sammy confessed with a sigh.

"Oh you are a dirty girl, aren't you?" His hand came down again, surprising Sammy with its intensity. "Did you suck her nipples?"

Sammy considered not answering, but when he raised his hand again she whispered, "Yes, and she sucked mine. And I rubbed my pussy against her leg, and she rubbed her cunt against my leg, and we both came and it was fabulous." The words exploded out in a rush when his hand came down again.

"You," he said as he slipped his finger between her legs to test her wetness, "are a nasty, dirty girl. Your pussy is drenched." His fingers slid enticingly over her slippery folds.

Damn, that felt good. Nick pulled his fingers from between her legs and smeared her slick juices all over her ass. Again and again he delved in, drawing her moisture out to cool the sweet burning in her ass. Sammy bucked against his touch, trying not to orgasm as he rubbed against her clit. It was too soon. This game had rules, unwritten rules that were unbreakable. He punished her for being naughty, and she pretended she didn't like it. *You dirty-minded bugger*, she thought, with a surge of affection for her husband. *You love hearing about this just as much as I love telling you.* She was so lost in the pleasure of his touch she nearly missed his next words.

"Did you eat her pussy? Did she suck on your hard little clit?"

"No. Oh, God I wanted to, but we ran out of time. We wanted to finish before you got back. To make you wonder." Oh, man, how she had wanted to taste Gina's pussy and feel Gina's tongue on her own. What a delight that would be—sweet heaven. She was getting hotter and wetter just thinking about it. Sammy writhed against Nick's hand, each slow sweep of his fingers driving her closer to orgasm.

"Are you going to see her again? Are you going to do her again?" Nick asked softly, dangerously. He increased the speed of his motions, his thumb rubbing her moist folds, two fingers dipping inside to drive her wild.

"Yes. Oh, God, yes." She didn't know if she meant she would see Gina again or if she was encouraging his actions. She really didn't care—she wanted, needed both. "Lunch, next week."

"Do you need to come?" Nick asked, stilling. "Are you hot just thinking about it? Do you need to play with your little girlfriend again, you nasty girl?" Sammy was without words—Nick's harsh words were driving her to the edge. "Tell me, my nasty little slut, do you need to come?" When Sammy could muster no more than a whimper, he added, "Come on, my slut, give me your cum. Come for me." He slammed his fingers in and out of her moist opening, taking her hard and rough, forcing her over the edge into a whirling world of delight.

*The Gift*

When she spiraled back down to reality, she was still dripping and ready for more. "Can I have your cock inside me?" she begged breathlessly. Damn, she needed him inside her. Playing with Gina had been incredible, but nothing beat a nice, hard cock shoved deep inside her. Especially when that cock belonged to the man she loved and couldn't live without. She pushed him back on the bed and climbed onto him, taking him inside her eager pussy in one smooth stroke. "Ah," she breathed as she sank down onto him fully.

"Damn, you are tight tonight," he praised, pumping into her. "I'm so glad you enjoyed your date, and I can't wait to hear about the next one."

"Touch my breasts." She needed to feel his rough hands grabbing and playing, teasing and stroking. He reached up and cupped her breasts in his hands, lifting them slightly and letting them drop back, as if testing their weight, watching intently as her nipples beaded into tight little balls.

Sammy felt his warm touch and pushed against his hands as she bounced on his thick, hard cock. Damn he filled her so well. He pinched her nipples, pulling and teasing a bit, giving a small touch of pain, not enough to really hurt, just enough to spur her arousal on. Each pinch sent a shiver of pleasure through her scalding pussy, and she bucked against him as he controlled her with the tips of his fingers. He pinched, and she pulled up and away, vainly trying to relieve the pressure. When he released her nipples, she slammed back down onto him, driving him deeper and deeper with each stroke until she was sure he couldn't possibly go any farther inside her.

His cock twitched inside her, each small movement pounding her insides, playing her like a drum and causing spasms to wrack through her body. She pumped harder—she was so close. Don't come yet. He's not ready. Wait for him. Come together. She chanted the words inside her head, trying to distract herself from the incredible rush of pleasure edging over her. She wanted to wait for Nick, to be together with him in that final peak. He swore, a harsh explicative exploding from his mouth as his cock swelled inside her. Grabbing her hips, he guided her motions, tilting her pelvis, controlling the angle and speed as he thrust into her, exploding as wave after wave of ecstasy ripped through him.

Sammy felt Nick's spasm and relished his harsh words. She could hear someone crying out and knew it was the sound of her own impending orgasm. She allowed him to guide her motions, and when he thrust into her one last time, she stopped resisting, stopped fighting, and let her orgasm overtake her very soul.

Slowly, she became aware of Nick's hands stroking her gently, soothing her sore ass, loving her body and cherishing her.

"Babe," he whispered, "I love you so damned much. I would be lost without you." Almost too weak to move, she slipped off him and nestled at Nick's side, her arm flung across his waist. He was hot, sticky, and sweaty, and she didn't care. His arm wrapped around her shoulder, pulling her close, his fingers lightly stroking her hair.

"That was fabulous," she panted in his ear. "Thank you."

Nick laughed, a soft, happy sound. It always made him laugh when she thanked him for her orgasms, but she couldn't help herself. He made her feel so good, so satisfied, loved and cherished that she found herself expressing her gratitude without thinking. "I love you, Nick Jarvis." Then she laughed. "You are one hell of a fuck."

♥♥♥

Over the next few days, the girls spent a lot of time together. They went to lunch, got manicures, went shopping. They had also made love to each other several times while Nick and Carl were at work or doing their own shopping. Each minute they spent together drew them closer until the afternoon that Sammy made a startling discovery.

She was falling in love with Gina. Not good friends love, but I need to spend the rest of my life with you love, and she was pretty sure she was feeling it for Carl too. The strong emotions made her nervous, but they made her feel good too. It took a lot of thought, as well as heart- and soul-searching, but at length she decided to embrace the emotions and accept them as part of who she was and what she needed.

"I need to talk to you," Sammy told Gina, sliding into the booth across from her at the local pub. They were seated at their usual table way in the back and were secluded from the prying eyes and ears of the other patrons.

Sammy saw Gina's eyes widen in panic. Oh, she thinks this is bad news. She smiled at Gina, who drew a slow, deep breath and released it.

After her fourth breath, Gina spoke. "Okay, shoot."

"I have a problem," Sammy blurted, twisting her hands together. She took a deep drink of the water Gina had ordered for her.

"Ye-e-a-a-ah," Gina responded, drawing the simple word out into five syllables.

"I think I love you," Sammy exploded, her face flushing with heat and color.

Gina squealed, jumped up, and hopped into the booth beside Sammy, wrapping her tight in her arms. "Oh, thank God." She laughed. "I love you too. I have since the first time I met you.

Oh, happy dance," she decreed, wiggling about. "I thought you were going to dump me."

Sammy laughed at Gina's exuberant tone. "But," she added, knowing she needed to get everything off her chest at once. Gina fell instantly motionless, her hands dropping to her lap with a thud.

"I think I want to fuck your husband," Sammy whispered worriedly. Gina's arms were back around her before she knew what was happening.

"Is that all?" She laughed loudly. "So fuck him. I don't mind." She kissed Sammy soundly on the lips. "He's my best guy, you're my best girl. What could be better?" She laughed again. "Well, Carl and you and me." She giggled, then her voice turned breathless. "Oh." Her voice was high and excited. "Carl and Nick and you and me. All at once."

Hot moisture flooded Sammy's sex, making it swell and throb. She could see them all together, teasing, playing, touching, and loving. She gasped in her excitement. Gina pulled back to stare at her, but before Gina could panic, Sammy blurted, "When?" and threw her arms around Gina, pulling her close. This was fabulous. She had a husband she loved more than anything, a girlfriend who was her lover, and soon she would add Carl to the mix. Did it get any better than this? Hell, no.

They spent the next couple of hours planning their strategy. Gina would seduce Nick, and Sammy would seduce Carl. They would make love separately before coming together as a group. While they had become a close-knit group over the past few weeks, there was always the chance that the electricity that ran through them all would fizzle when put to the acid test.

*The Gift*

# CHAPTER EIGHT

Sammy stood behind Carl where he sat at the table after lunch. Gina had already lured Nick away on the pretext of showing him the perfect gift for Sammy. She rubbed his shoulder and neck for a moment, delighting in the play of his muscles under her hands and in his groans of pleasure. She varied her touch from relaxation to seduction and back.

"The mall?" Carl complained to Sammy. "You want me to go to the mall with you? It's only days until Christmas. Couldn't we just go to the hardware store? I know he wants a saws-all."

"Stop whining, you big baby." She kissed the top of his head and flicked her tongue across his ear. "Please," she whispered, her breath soft and teasing against his skin. "I'll make it worth your while." She pulled out all the stops, pressing her breasts against the back of his neck in a blatant come-on. Just being near him was turning her on. He smelled so nice, like spice and man, and he had all those muscles just waiting for her to caress them.

"Fine," he groused. "Let's get this over with, and you owe me. Big time!" He turned in his chair, pulled her into his lap, and devoured her mouth with his.

Oh, he tasted like coffee and strawberry waffles. Who knew that would make such an intoxicating combination? She ran her tongue across his lips, reveling in their firm, rough texture. He was so like Nick—they both had full, firm lips—and so unlike Gina with her soft sexy mouth.

They walked through the mall, hand in hand. Carl kept trying to pull his hand free, but Sammy wanted to touch him. As they walked, she traced little circles against his knuckles to keep his mind on her promise. When she entered a high-end lingerie shop, he hesitated.

"Don't be a chicken." She tugged on his arm, urging him forward. "This will only take a minute." She greeted the twenty-something clerk by name. "Hi, Erin. This is Carl. He's the friend I told you about earlier." Erin greeted them both with a quick hug and a wide smile. "Is my stuff ready?" Sammy asked, heading toward the far corner of the store.

"Absolutely." Erin laughed. "I've put you in room seven. Upstairs. None of the other rooms are booked," she clarified with another tinkling laugh. "Have fun, Carl." With an envious look at Sammy she added, "I wish I were you."

Tugging the worried and reluctant Carl behind her, Sammy headed upstairs. She gave each of the open rooms a cursory glance to be sure they were all empty, pulled him into room seven, and flipped the dead bolt behind them.

"What the hell is this?" he asked, staring around him at the spacious room. One side had a straight-backed chair, a comfortable looking chaise lounge, and an end table with a jug of ice water and two glasses on it. There was also a stool, a cloth and wood room divider, and a rack of clothing. A door to the left was slightly open, revealing a bathroom complete with shower. "I didn't even know this place had an upstairs." He ranged around, taking it all in before whirling to confront her. "What the hell is going on?" he demanded.

Sammy pushed a finger against his chest, gently steering him toward the chaise. "Exactly what I told you. I picked out some things for Nick for Christmas, and I want you to help me choose the right ones. Sit," she demanded with one last shove. "I'll be right back."

She slipped behind the curtain and stripped off her clothing as quickly as she could. She had to get this started before he panicked and bolted, or before she lost her nerve entirely. She grabbed the first item off the rack. Perfect. Erin had laid them out in the right order. With a brisk economy of motion, she slipped into a virginal white bra and panty set, then slid on the matching silk stockings and garter belt and slid her feet into a pair of jeweled stilettos.

Carl was standing in front of the chaise looking slightly panicked as he peered around the room, clearly seeking an escape route. She walked slowly toward him, swiveling her hips and mussing her hair. "Hey, lover," she purred, pushing him back onto the chaise with one touch of her finger. He flopped down and sat staring at her, his mouth making small, flapping motions as if he were trying to say something. She bit back a smile of power. This was fun.

She pivoted on her heel and showed him the back of the outfit. Looking back over her shoulder, she stared at him until he met her eyes. The frantic look had changed to a glaze of arousal. Good. "So," she asked coyly. "What do you think of this outfit?" She slid one hand down an exposed hip and caressed her backside where it showed under the short panties. She circled her hips the way she'd learned in her "strip-a-cise" class and spun slowly around. Placing her hands on either side of his head, she leaned toward him, giving him a good view of her cleavage where it swelled over the low cups of the bra, her nipples playing hide and seek with his eyes. "Do you think Nick'll like it?" she teased and spun around slowly, giving him a full view of the entire outfit. When his breathing increased and his face flushed, she knew she had him.

Placing one heel on the chaise alongside his thigh, she leaned in again. "Well? No answer? Maybe he'd like something different. Maybe in pink." She trailed her finger along his cheek before sashaying her way back to the dressing room. As she skittered out of the first outfit and into the second, she thought she heard him swear.

"Damn," Carl swore lowly and adjusted his cock in his jeans. He was as hard as a rock. What the hell was Sammy up to? He wondered. There had to be more to this than shopping for Nick. Oh hell, he thought, let this be going where I want it to.

Sammy reappeared wearing some filmy thing in pale pink. It was short, and when she pivoted before him, still wearing the white stockings and shoes, he could see half her ass under the double layers of chiffon. He grunted under his breath. He was not going to let her get the best of him.

Then it hit him. Gina was in on this, the naughty little minx. She had sent him to see Sammy, saying she needed help with a gift. They had set him up. He smiled to himself. This was going to be fun.

Sammy read the resistance in his eyes and knew it was temporary at best. She cupped her breasts in her hands as if to offer them for his pleasure. "I kind of like pink, don't you?" she asked, turning and bending from the waist to place her hands on the floor. Her ass was displayed before him, her legs spread so wide he could almost see her dark, puckered sphincter and pussy around the miniscule thong that ran between her legs. "Do you like pink?" she asked again, pumping her hips a bit. She straightened slowly, one vertebra at a time, and turned to face him. She cupped his face in her hands and gave him a quick peck on the mouth. "Guess not," she quipped. "Maybe green."

She sauntered into the small space behind the divider, whipped off the outfit and playfully threw it over the divider in his direction. This time she clearly heard the expletive he muttered. She wasn't worried about the clothing—she'd already paid for all the outfits after Gina helped her pick them out. Her frequent large purchases at this store allowed her the privilege of renting the upstairs for the afternoon. She had played this game once before with Nick and had loved it just as much then as she did now with Carl.

The next outfit took a moment longer to change into, so she kept up a running monologue about how much she loved the feel of silk and lace against her skin. As she slipped into the boy briefs and straightened them out, her finger brushed her pussy, and she was startled by how wet she was already. She took a second to stroke her clit, loving the feel of her moist femininity throbbing against her hand.

At last she stepped into the black and silver pumps and strode cheekily from the room. "What do you think?"

She stood before Carl, hands on her hips, legs spread apart. She thrust her hips at him, revealing that she was naked under the short, floating top of emerald lace. He stared at her without answering. A bit miffed by his stoic response, she put one black heel alongside him on the cushion, and with a quick double hop placed the other leg beside him as well. Standing there, she straddled him, her pussy just inches from his mouth. "No opinion?" she demanded, and thrust her hips forward to ensure he could smell her arousal.

When he sucked in a breath and let out a long sigh, she knew she had him beat. There was no longer any doubt in her mind. She had won this round. She cupped her breasts, then slid her hands down her sides, caressing and teasing, pausing with her fingers interlaced over her pubic mound.

"I kind of like this one, don't you?" She slid her fingers lower, spreading her lips apart so Carl could see how wet and aroused she was.

"Glurk," was his only response, but his hands clutched her ankles.

"Aw, come on, Carl. Don't you like this one?" she teased, tapping her clit with her finger. "Give me an answer and I'll let you touch it." She rubbed her mound in slow circles before holding her slippery fingers in front of his mouth.

"Yes, dammit," he snapped at her, grabbing her hand and sucking the juices from her fingers. "Damn, you taste so sweet." He leaned toward her, trying to get a direct taste.

She hopped down and waggled a finger at him. "Tsk tsk," she teased. "What color do you think Nick would like?" Her tone was pure seduction.

"Black. Nick likes black lace, but I like red. Put on the red one." His voice was thick with arousal and pleaded just a little.

Sammy leaned down and kissed him full on the lips. "For you? Anything, Big Guy." She ran a hand across the impressive bulge in his pants and skipped past the rack, grabbing the red outfit and changing quickly.

"Carl," she called from behind the screen, "do you like these boots?" She stuck one leg from behind the screen, revealing tight, black leather boots that came up to her thighs. They were her new come-fuck-me boots, and she loved the way they caressed her legs, making her look as hot and slutty as she felt.

"Fuck, yeah," he groaned, his hand massaging his cock through his pants. He was a goner, and he knew it. There was no sense resisting any longer. Obviously Sammy was intent on seducing him, and he was going to let her. He undid his belt and opened his jeans to allow more room for growth.

Sammy stepped slowly from behind the divider and stopped to strike a sexy pose, one hand cupping her breast, the other on her hip, legs akimbo and hair flung back. She smiled when she realized his erection was making an impressive bulge in his underwear and was peeking out of his open jeans. "What do you think?" She gestured toward her tight, red corset that laced up the front with black satin ribbon. Trimmed all the way around with white faux fur, it came low on her hips, but stopped to reveal a thin line of tanned skin above the miniscule scrap that passed for panties. The front of the panties was red silk, while the back was fake white fur to match the trim around the edges of the corset. Black silk stockings peeked over the top of the boots, held in place by red garters. The corset was laced so tightly she could barely draw a full breath, but it thrust her breasts together and up over the cups at the top.

"Holy Mary, Mother of God," he groaned when he saw her standing there. "That is about the hottest fucking outfit I have ever seen. Get your sweet ass over here."

"Don't you want to see it all?" She pivoted slowly, just out of reach. Most of her ass was showing, and it made his mouth water. She had an extremely naughty Mrs. Claus look happening, and he loved it.

"Come here," he demanded before adding a soft, "please."

She pivoted a bit more before moving to stand in front of him. "Oh, don't you look uncomfortable. Let me help you with that." She knelt before him and helped him wiggle out of his jeans and into a condom. Moving to straddle him, she sat down on his lap, his cock banging at the silk standing sentry over the entrance to her body. She paused a moment to slide the silk aside then slammed herself down onto his cock, fully engulfing him to the base of his shaft in one smooth stroke.

"Damn," he swore with an upward buck of his hips. "How can you be so wet and tight at the same time?"

"Baby, I want you bad," she replied, moving herself up and down slowly, stroking the full length of him with her inner muscles clenched tight. "Touch my breasts," she pleaded, placing his hands where she wanted them.

"Yes." He trailed his fingers along the upped edge of the corset, teasing her with soft strokes and gentle caresses. She grabbed his hands and pressed them harder against her, crushing her breasts with the pressure. She bucked hard atop him and pleaded, "Damn you, Carl, I've waited a long time for this. Save the gentle for next time." She guided his hands to show how she wanted it. Obediently, he roughened his touch without actually hurting her and watched her eyes darken with desire.

"Yes," she cried, pumping frantically on him as he tweaked her nipples and pulled on them, his nails digging into the sensitive flesh.

He suckled one nipple and caressed her ass while she rode him, her frantic motions matching his. She rode him hard, and he loved every second of it, his cock thrilling when her breasts swelled and her nipples hardened even further before she cried out, took his mouth in a harsh kiss, and exploded.

In her release, she gripped him so tightly he could barely thrust into her. He pumped once, twice, and on the third stroke slammed home and stayed pressed against her, shouting her name as he exploded inside her.

When he came back to reality, he realized they were still locked together, his shrinking cock still deep inside her spasming pussy. She kissed him again, this time more gently, nuzzling and teasing, her lips soft and gentle. Carl wrapped his arms around Sammy, pulling her close and enjoying her soft kisses. "Damn, that was fantastic," he breathed against her lips. "I could learn to love a woman who treats me like that."

Sammy stilled on top of him. "Good." She took a deep breath. "Carl, I think I'm falling in love with you. And Gina." He looked startled, and she knew a moment of panic. Fuck, she thought. Too soon. I've gone and scared him off.

Sammy could tell her confession startled him, but to her surprise, he didn't seem scared.

He looked her in the eye and smiled. "I think I love you, too." It wasn't the full confession that most women would want to hear, but Sammy was pleased and began kissing him in earnest, her breasts rubbing against his chest as she moved against him. His cock slipped free of her body, and she quickly removed the condom, tossing it aside before straddling him again.

"Babe," she whispered excitedly as she felt his cock stirring to life under her and began to swivel her hips enticingly.

## CHAPTER NINE

Gina met Nick at her place. Like Sammy, she was using the Christmas gift ruse. Gina had told Nick she had the perfect gift for him to give Sammy. Nick settled on the sofa, and Gina brought him a beer. They shared some idle talk for a few minutes, but something about the way Gina was acting put Nick on edge. She seemed twitchy and wouldn't quite meet his eye, and over the past few weeks he had grown accustomed to her blatant come-on looks. Today she seemed nervous or something and he wondered what was up.

Finally he asked her. "Gina, stop fluttering around and tell me what this is all about. Obviously you didn't bring me here to show me a gift for Sammy." He stared directly at her, pinning her with his look.

## *The Gift*

She cleared her throat, started to speak, then fell silent and cleared her throat again. He gave her a raised eyebrow. "Listen, honey," he warned her, "I've had about my fill of this game, whatever this game might be."

She flushed and confessed. "Sammy asked me to bring you here. She asked me to distract you for a while." She refused to meet his eyes again.

Nick assumed her reluctance was due to the Christmas gift charade and let her off the hook. "So, distract me, then," he challenged her with a waggle of his eyebrows.

"More beer? Coffee, tea?"

"Isn't the expression coffee, tea, or me?" he teased.

"Would you like it to be?" Gina asked quietly, as if unsure of offending him.

Nick reached out, snagged her by the arm, and pulled her into his lap. She sat there, straddling the growing bulge bumping against her groin. Nick pulled her to him and kissed her deeply. "Mm," he replied into her lips. "But I'm a married man, and no matter how hot you make me, I won't betray Sammy."

Gina was up off his lap like a shot. "You won't betray her—is that your only reason for refusing me?" Gina asked seriously.

"Well, that and the fact Carl is my best friend," Nick responded candidly. "But I know he wouldn't begrudge me the taste of your fine pussy."

Gina pulled an envelope out of her back pocket and handed it to him. His name was scrawled on the front in Sammy's familiar chicken scratch. While he pulled the note out, Gina disappeared down the hallway toward her bedroom, and he wondered briefly what she was up to.

*Nick,*

*I know we are married, but I also know that you want Gina. You told me yourself. You gave her to me like I asked and now I am returning the favor and giving her to you. Make love to her, like you do to me. Make her feel good. And while you are doing that, think about me fucking Carl, 'cause that's where I'll be while you are playing with Gina's tight little pussy. I know you and Carl have shared women in the past, and I know you won't mind sharing me as well.*

*Enjoy yourself and know I love you.*

*Sammy*

Nick stared at the note in disbelief. He read it a second time and a third before the words sank in. "Holy fuck," he exclaimed, jumping to his feet. He had carte blanche to fool around with his best friend's girl, and he fully intended to do that. Here and now!

When he got to the bedroom, the lights were off and the room lit by the soft glow of candles. The air smelled of woman and soft floral perfume. Gina was laying spread eagle on the bed wearing nothing but her skin and a look of invitation. His hand dropped to his crotch, and he stroked his burgeoning cock through his pants while he looked his fill.

She was about the same height as Sammy, maybe five three, and slender. She had small breasts, hardly more than an A-cup, and his eyes devoured them like a starving man gobbled up a meal. Her legs were long and lithe, her pussy waxed clean and glistening in the subdued light. Her hair was long and black and fanned out around her on the pillows. As he stood there studying her from the top of her head to the tip of her sexy, painted toes, he stroked himself again. While he watched, she began touching herself, running her hands up and down her midriff and ribcage before moving to cup her breasts and tease her nipples.

"Come on, Nick." She writhed on the bed. "I need you. Come play with me." She pivoted until she was facing him, her ass in the air, her elbows on the bed, and her long hair draping over her shoulders to hide her breasts. She crawled toward him until she reached the edge of the bed. She stayed there on all fours and gestured for him to come closer. "Come here, big boy," she teased. "I can't wait to taste your cock." She shifted around a bit, her gaze never leaving the bulge in his pants.

It was a good thing Nick had no intention of refusing her, because he wasn't sure he would have possessed the willpower to resist her. He yanked his shirt over his head and stripped off his jeans, shorts and socks in one motion. He stayed in the doorway, his hand lightly pumping his erection, teasing her. She wiggled her ass again, and he moved to stand in front of her, so close his cock tapped her on the nose.

Without warning or preamble, Gina opened her mouth and engulfed the head of his cock. Immediately she began licking and sucking. The first touch of her mouth was electric—she was so soft and wet and damned hot. Nick bucked under her gentle touches, and she started pumping her mouth up and down in earnest.

He reached out to steady her head in his hands and began pumping back. Not hard, just moving in and out of the moist heat of her mouth with slow, sure strokes. He moved with relish, enjoying each motion and the feel of her lips to the fullest. At least he did until she started flicking her tongue along his length and around the head of his cock. Unable to stop himself he plunged deeply, harshly into her mouth.

She reached one hand up and grabbed his ass, her fingers digging in as she urged him on, making him pump harder and faster. He plunged in all the way, his cock banging against the back of her throat, and he felt her gag against him. Easing off a bit, he pumped hard, but not so deeply. She dug her nails into his ass again, urging him on, begging him without words to take her mouth hard and fast and deep. Surprised by the urging, he paused a moment. Sammy liked sucking him, but didn't seem interested in having him take her mouth roughly. Nick stared down at Gina, and she backed up, allowing his cock to slip from her mouth. She flipped over to lie on her back, her head hanging over the edge of the bed.

"Come on, Nicky," she purred. "Fuck my mouth." She licked her lips and smiled up at him. "Hard."

The blatant invitation was more than he could resist, and Nick slipped his throbbing cock back into her waiting mouth. The angle was different, allowing him to plunge deeper than before. He pumped slowly and watched as she cupped and squeezed her breasts, tweaking her nipples and pulling gently on them, all the while licking his cock and milking it with her mouth. Slowly he increased his pace and depth, worried about choking her or hurting her, but the harder and deeper he pumped, the more she wiggled on the bed, one hand furiously rubbing her pussy, the other teasing her breasts. She bucked and twisted, her mouth working its magic on his erection.

Nick grasped her gently by the hair and held her head still as he increased his pace. He was quickly losing control, his balls tightening and leg muscles twitching with the effort to hold back his release. He pumped hard, his hands holding her head still as he drove into her harder and harder. He banged against the back of her throat, felt her spasm around him, her throat pulsing. She rubbed her pussy frantically with both hands, her mouth working him eagerly, sucking and swallowing him in deeply. He drove himself home, his cock bumping the back of her throat. Gina's hips pumped into the air, and she groaned around his cock, her orgasm taking them both by surprise and tipping Nick over the edge. He bucked against her, pulling back slightly, his release flooding her mouth.

Gina relaxed her throat and opened her mouth wide as Nick pumped into her. His cock tasted divine. He was musky and masculine and perfectly delicious. She fondled her breasts, rubbing with just the right amount of pressure and teasing to pull her toward her release. She loved this. There was nothing sweeter than the feeling of a man lodged deep in her throat, her breathing hampered but not stopped as he bucked and pumped into her. There was a special feeling of giving and of power in knowing she had his release in the palm of her hands and controlled it.

♥♥♥

Nick pumped deeper into her mouth and she slid both hands down her body to cup her pussy. She was so hot, so wet and aroused that she knew she was going to lose the battle to hold back her orgasm. She flicked his head with her tongue once more, and Nick slammed deep into her mouth, the spasms of his release shivering up the length of his cock. It was more than she could take, and she exploded into orgasm, choking slightly before swallowing his load.

Nick spasmed into Gina's mouth again and again. His semen flooded her mouth and flowed out down her face even though she swallowed, valiantly trying to take it all. At long last, he was totally spent. He pulled his softening cock from her mouth and leaned down to kiss her.

Gina lifted her head to meet Nick's mouth. For a moment she was surprised that he kissed her on the mouth so soon after coming in it. Most men would shy away from tasting their own cum. Then she remembered that Nick and Carl had a history of loving each other. Nick was no stranger to the taste of sperm, and somehow she found the thought that Nick might have tasted her boyfriend's sperm very erotic.

They kissed for a long, sweet moment before Nick moved to help her fully onto the bed. He eased her head onto the bed and slid a pillow beneath it before lying down beside her and drawing her close into his embrace.

They lay together, nestled together like two spoons in a drawer, Nick's arm around her, idly toying with Gina's nipples. Her hand reached backward to stroke his thigh where he pressed up against her backside. "Keep doing that," she whispered, "and you'll have me ready to go again in no time." His cock twitched against her ass in response, and she felt him growing hard, his cock pulsing against her as it came back to life.

She rolled over, squishing her breast against his chest and grinding her mound against his erection. "My, my," she teased. "Now, what is this?" She bucked gently against him and laughed at his groan of submission before pushing him over onto his back and swinging her leg over him. In one fluid motion, she was straddling him, her moist pussy teasing the head of his cock before allowing him to slip inside.

*The Gift*

# CHAPTER TEN

Christmas Eve was upon them before they knew it. Sammy stood in the bedroom, looking into the mirror and primping her hair. She would wear it up tonight, she decided—that would allow her to tease the men by taking it down and looking all sexily rumpled. Gina and Carl were coming over later for drinks and appetizers. What Carl and Nick didn't know was that Sammy planned to seduce them both, along with Gina, under the Christmas tree.

The past few weeks had been a whirlwind of excitement for the two couples. As always, Christmas meant a round of office and house parties and endless hours of entertainment. Somehow, in spite of their hectic schedules, they had managed to find time to spend together. Sometimes it was just two or three of them, and occasionally it was all four. Each time they got together they became closer and now, on the eve of Christmas, they were like family. Deep inside, Sammy held onto the hope that they would join each other and live as a family with all four of them sharing one house and spending all their spare time together loving and caring for each other.

She had another secret hope as well. Gradually, she had come to suspect that Nick and Carl were lovers, and that they had been for some time. Probably since long before Sammy came on the scene. She also suspected Gina had known all along. Initially, she wasn't sure what had tipped her off to their history. Maybe it was the easy camaraderie the two men shared, or perhaps all the casual touches that seemed to have an intimacy deeper than just friendship. It had taken a lot of thought to come to terms with the unusual nature of the relationship between the two men.

Initially, it had made her uncomfortable and a little jealous. But eventually she came to the realization that the thought of watching Carl and Nick make love to each other turned her on. She began having dreams of catching them together and watching them in secret. Soon those thoughts progressed to fantasies of joining them. Just this morning, she had awoken from visions of watching Nick and Carl together while she was cuddled in Gina's arms. Tonight she was going to make that happen. She just wasn't sure how—yet.

She slid into her sexy Santa lingerie and slipped a comfortable, button-front dress over the top. The black leather knee boots she had modeled for Carl completed her outfit and turned it from ordinary to sultry. From the outside, she looked like she did every other day, but as she looked in the mirror she realized something was different. She had a glow to her skin. She looked...alive and excited. She gave herself one last squirt of perfume before heading downstairs.

As she traveled down the few steps, she was struck by the memory of her first time with Gina just weeks ago. She had descended these very steps knowing Gina was going to be there, but unaware of her incredible bisexuality. Things sure could change for the better in no time at all. As she entered the kitchen, her happiness bubbled over, and she laughed aloud.

Nick turned to look at her and couldn't help but share her happiness. He pulled her into his arms and kissed her deeply. She was different lately. He had known his wife had a high sex drive and had always loved that about her. When she'd expressed her desire to love a woman, he had been surprised and thrilled all at once. When she gave him permission to be with Gina, it was more than he could have hoped for. He reached down to cup her ass and drag her hard against his stiffening cock.

She looked up at him and asked, "You didn't mind me telling you about how I seduced Carl, did you?" She glanced away, a little bit shy and unsure of his answer.

"Hell, no," he replied with a swat to her bottom. "I love hearing about how slutty you are. Nothing makes me hotter than you telling me about sex, talking dirty." He thrust his erection against her belly. "Well, nothing except fucking you." His hands pulled her dress up so he could caress her ass. Her furry ass?

"What the hell," he blurted, blinking down at her. "Your ass is furry."

Sammy giggled and backed out of his embrace, waggling her finger at him. "You weren't supposed to be touching my ass. Forget you went there," she advised him. "You'll get to see later."

"What the hell are you wearing?" he asked, doing his best to corner her and get his hands back under her skirt to reveal her secret. "New lingerie?" He dropped to his knees in front of her and stroked his hands up and down her boots.

"Just you never mind. Go start a fire in the fireplace and open some wine." She nudged him away with her knee, laughing as he fell with a mock gasp to the floor, trying to look up her dress. "Naughty boy." She shook her finger at him. "Do as you're told before I decide you never get to see what's under this dress." She walked around behind him, placed a booted heel on his ass, and kicked him toward the living room.

"Yes, Mistress. As you wish, Mistress." He crawled on all fours until he was out of the room.

Before long, Sammy could hear the strains of Christmas music coming through the door and Nick banging around in the fireplace. They had chosen to leave the fireplace as a wood-burning one. They both loved the crackle and pop as the logs burned.

Singing softly along with the music, Sammy danced around the kitchen, preparing the snacks for later and thinking about making love to her friends. She had made love with all three of them separately. Nick was strong and loving and always knew when to lead and when to follow. Gina was soft and enticing, with an innate ability to sense what Sammy wanted. Carl was all man and loved it hard and fast. Tonight, Sammy wanted them all together, if she could just figure out a way to make it happen.

Carl and Gina arrived right on time, quickly slipped out of their warm jackets, and settled before the fire with a drink. Carl and Nick each sat in a chair while Sammy cuddled with Gina on the couch. It had become a habit when the four of them were together—the girls always cuddled together, and the men sat a precise eighteen inches apart. It made Sammy want to laugh to see how careful they were to avoid touching each other when someone else was looking. But when they thought they were alone, the two men couldn't keep their hands off each other.

They shared a few snacks and a few laughs over old times, and eventually Sammy decided that the guys had consumed just enough alcohol to lower their resistance. Leaning into Gina, Sammy began planting small, soft kisses up and down her neckline. She nibbled her ear before trailing her mouth lower toward the scoop neck of Gina's silken top. She snuck a quick glance at the guys to be sure they were watching.

They were. Both men were staring wide-eyed at the action before them. That the women were regular lovers was not a surprise—that they would start something in front of both men was shocking. They hadn't touched each other publicly since their first night together.

Gina returned Sammy's kisses and let her hands wander up and down Sammy's body, cupping her generous breasts and caressing them softly before moving on to play in her hair or stroke the soft planes of her abdomen. Briefly she wondered what Sammy was up to and then decided she didn't care. There was something really hot about making out in front of Nick and Carl, knowing they wished they could participate. She kissed and fondled Sammy for a few minutes before Sammy whispered in her ear. They whispered excitedly back and forth for a time, their hands moving idly while they conversed.

As one, they leaned back from each other and rose to their feet. Sammy moved to straddle Nick's lap, and Gina settled herself on Carl's. In unison, they each cupped their own breasts and held them toward their men like offerings, inviting them to touch.

Nick threw a startled glance at Sammy, then at Carl, when the ladies settled themselves down and offered themselves up. Something was going on, and as enticing as the sight before him was, he felt a slight shiver of trepidation. Sammy was up to something, and he sure wished he knew what it was. He worried a moment before deciding to go with the flow. Whatever naughty thing she was planning would come on her terms, and there was no sense worrying about it.

Sammy leaned in and started kissing Nick deeply. When they at last came up for air, he noticed Gina and Carl were following suit. Sammy's leg twitched against Nick's, and she leaned toward Gina. Their lips met, and they shared a long, deep kiss. Grinding down on the men's laps, they began caressing each other again.

Nick looked at Carl, and they shared a smile. So this was the game, was it? Their lovely ladies wanted to play as a foursome. The men shared a silent high-five, and when their hands came down, they stayed joined together on the couch between them.

For several long, enticing moments they sat together, enjoying the heated pressure of the ladies writhing in their laps as they loved each other. Almost as if sharing a thought, each man raised his other hand to begin touching the bounty before him.

Sammy stole a quick glance at the men and happily noted they were holding hands. Perfect. Things were coming along nicely. Releasing Gina, Sammy slid off Nick's lap and moved to drag the coffee table out of her way. She slid it across the hardwood floor into a corner and spread a thick quilt on the floor. Tugging on Nick's hand, she drew him down onto the blanket, even as Gina followed her lead and drew Carl down to lay beside Nick.

Sammy straddled Carl, and Gina moved to sit on top of Nick. The girls shared a glance, and in one smooth motion pulled their dresses over their heads, revealing their matching undergarments. They were wearing tight red corsets that laced up the front with black ribbon. They were laced so tight even Gina's small breasts seemed to spill over the top enticingly. The corsets were trimmed with white faux fur that matched the backs of their panties. Black silk stockings and red garters completed the outfits. The only difference was that Gina wore stilettos and Sammy wore skin-tight, thigh-high leather boots. Perched on top of the men, they made a striking pair.

Gina's long dark hair contrasted nicely with Sammy's riot of blonde curls. Sammy's large breasts seemed to beg to touch Gina's smaller ones. Nick groaned aloud at the delectable sight. Damned if he didn't love both these women. He shared a smile with Carl and knew at that moment that it simply didn't get better than this. Here he was on Christmas Eve with the three people he loved most in the whole world. Suddenly keeping his love for Carl a secret didn't matter anymore. He wanted to share this grand feeling with Sammy and with Gina.

Pivoting slightly, he grabbed Carl's hand and tugged gently. Without dislodging Gina, Nick rose on one elbow, facing Carl, and stared down at him, raising one eyebrow. Carl copied his motion and rose to meet him, their lips coming together in a soft, deep kiss.

Sammy stared at the men as they shared a kiss and felt a huge, wet shudder of desire wash through her. She turned toward Gina, drawing her close for a kiss. Gina's breath was coming in soft, panting gasps, and Sammy knew she was aroused by the sight before them. Their lips met on a sigh. Their hands began wandering, and Sammy felt the firm touch of Carl's hand on her thigh and the sudden increase in the size of his erection where it pressed against the soft fabric of her panties, pushing them into her moist folds. Suddenly ravenous, she slid off Carl and started working at his belt and the fly of his pants. She needed him inside her. Now!

Gina sucked in a breath of disappointment when Sammy moved away from her, breaking their contact, but when she saw Sammy fumbling at Carl's waist, she quickly followed suit and began the delightful task of disrobing Nick. Her fingers fumbled a bit in her haste and excitement. She wanted this, wanted to make love to the three of them at once. It took only seconds to strip Nick bare and impale herself on his hard shaft. She slid down onto him, engulfing him to the base in one smooth, hard stroke.

Sammy perched over Carl's naked groin, her slick folds hovering at the tip of his cock. She rubbed back and forth for a moment, moistening his head with her arousal before allowing it to slide inside her. Slowly, with precision that nearly drove her out of her mind, she lowered herself inch by inch onto his erection. He was long and hard and more than ready. He bucked against her, driving the last couple of inches home in one sharp thrust. She ground against him, taking him in fully, reveling in the feel of his rough arousal rubbing against her smooth, waxed lips.

She paused a moment, enjoying the feeling of fullness, and began to work her hips in slow circles. She moved in a tiny circle, lifting slightly with each motion until she was traveling around and around and up and down at the same time. Beside her, she heard a gasp and turned to see Gina throw her head back in abandon as the first orgasm overcame her. She was beautiful in her release; her breasts thrust forward, nipples hard and begging. One hand was braced on Nick's chest, the other reaching out to clasp Sammy's hand. Nick had one hand on Gina's waist, guiding her motions, while the other was still tangled with Carl's. Gina's mouth was open as she panted and whimpered. Sammy thought it was the loveliest sight she had ever witnessed.

Sammy looked down at Nick and was surprised to see his gaze pivoting between her, Gina and Carl. It was as if he couldn't decide who he wanted to watch. Still holding Gina's hand in her own, Sammy brought her hands up to cup her breasts as she ground down on Carl. Gina pulled her hand free, and Sammy felt a tingling trail of fire where Gina's questing fingers trailed along her side to cup Sammy's ass. She squeezed tightly, the firm pinch setting off Sammy's orgasm. She sucked in a startled breath, rose up and slammed back down, driving Carl's cock deep inside her moist core, grinding her clit against him, the pleasure almost too intense to bear, and her world exploded around her.

Sammy pumped slowly as she returned to earth, and looking down at Nick she spoke softly. "Kiss him again. I want to see you together."

One simple statement and Nick knew what Sammy was up to. This wasn't just about making love as a group. She knew he and Carl were lovers. He wondered if she realized the full extent of what that meant. He kissed Carl deeply before speaking. "I don't think you know what that means," he warned her. "It's not kind or gentle." He kissed Carl again, releasing his hand and touching Carl's chest.

"I don't care," Sammy vowed. "I want to see you make love to him." She leaned in, and they shared a three-way kiss.

"Not fair," Gina complained lightly, trying to squeeze her face in to join the kiss. Her motions knocked Sammy off balance, and she grasped at Gina for support as she went over. Instead of steadying herself, she managed to topple them both over. They laughed a bit and turned their attention back to the men.

"Come on, guys," Sammy pleaded. "I want to watch."

"We want to watch," Gina corrected as she righted herself alongside Sammy.

"Make love," they pleaded together.

Both men groaned. "It's not making love," Nick warned them.

"It's fucking," Carl growled.

"Fucking good," Nick confessed, pushing Carl onto his knees. "Don't say we didn't warn you," Nick threatened, using his saliva to lubricate Carl's ass. He applied some spit to the head of his cock and rubbed it against Carl's tight anus. "I am going to fuck you good."

He swiveled his hips a bit and slid the tip of his cock inside. Carl stiffened under him and with a jerk drove himself backward, his ass engulfing Nick's entire length in one harsh motion. Both men gasped and groaned as they began to pump harshly against each other.

Sammy was shocked. She didn't know what she had been expecting—something softer, maybe—certainly not this animal coupling. But as she watched them fuck each other, Nick's hand pumping Carl's pulsing cock, she realized she was becoming aroused again. She felt Gina pushing against her and fell onto her back. With a wiggle of her hips, she slid under Carl. Sammy pushed Nick's hand away and took Carl's cock into her mouth. Carl stilled his motions and allowed her to pump her mouth up and down his shaft while Nick slammed into him from behind.

Sammy felt Gina's soft hands on her thighs, urging them apart, spreading them wide as she settled herself between them. The first touch of Gina's tongue on her slit was electric, and Sammy's hips jerked up to grind against her friend's soft mouth. Gina wiggled around a bit until she was half kneeling, half lying on top of Sammy, her pussy close enough for Sammy to touch.

Lying on her back, Carl's erection in her mouth, Sammy gave herself to sensation. She reveled in the motion of Carl's hips as Nick slammed into him and in the hot, moist pressure of Gina's pussy as it ground against her hand, mimicking the action of

Gina's tongue on her clit. Nick shouted out his release, causing Carl's cock to swell and explode in Sammy's mouth. Gina frantically licked Sammy's clit, and Sammy gave in to the waves of pleasure that threatened to swamp her. As she reached her release, she was vaguely aware of the familiar sounds of Gina's orgasm.

It was a long while before any of them found the energy to extract themselves from the pile of satiated flesh on the floor. They lay there, softly stroking and kissing each other, half on the floor, half on the quilt. The floor was hard and unforgiving, but none of them cared.

"Merry Christmas," Sammy murmured, her voice filled with satisfaction and happiness.

"Hell, yeah," Nick agreed.

"Merry Christmas," Gina sighed.

"Babe," was all Carl could muster, making the others laugh.

They were silent for a while, each lost in their own happy thoughts.

"I have an idea," Sammy said at last. "I love all you guys so much." She took a deep breath before going on. "I think we should all live together." She waited a breathless moment while the others absorbed her words.

"Damned skippy," Gina agreed.

"Fucking rights." Nick gave a fist pump in the air.

"Yeah," groaned Carl, his voice laden with exhaustion.

Sammy bounced to her knees and gave each of them a quick hug. "Damned if this isn't the best Christmas present ever." She giggled and everyone laughed.

"Merry Christmas," she whispered, her voice light with a smile.

## EXERPT: Tessa's Trio

"You know that I'm only going under protest," Tessa reminded her long-time friend. "I hate bars. I hate parties, and frankly I'm not all that thrilled about men right now." She crossed her arms over her chest and glared. Becky's laughter surprised Tessa.

"You are such a liar." Becky shook her finger in Tessa's face. "You like going to bars and dancing. You love parties, and more than that, you love men. You're just pissed that Rick cheated on you and you had to dump him. He won't be there, I checked. He's gone to Mexico with that new skank of his." Turning back to the mirror Becky ran a brush through her short black hair, spritzed a bit of hairspray into it and straightened her large breasts inside her bra before declaring herself done. "Now, get over here and we'll have you ready in no time."

"I…don't…want…to…go," she repeated.

"Yes…you…do. And you damn well know it. I can't figure out why you are protesting. Everyone will be there. We'll have a couple of beers, some conversation, some unwinding, all followed by a good night's sleep. It's the perfect way to end a stupidly long day." She crooked a finger at her friend who heaved a huge sigh and sat down at the dressing table. "We won't mess with your hair." She touched a corkscrew curl with a hint of reverence. "Every woman I know would kill for this hair."

Tessa smiled at her friend's generous compliment. It was true; her hair was her best feature. She studied herself in the mirror. Her hair fell to just past her shoulders in perfect corkscrew curls of golden brown, and in the sun it shone with red highlights. She didn't know which ancestor has gifted her with her curls rather than her sister's poker-straight, fine hair, but she thanked them. She inherited the best hair; her sister got the generous, sexy breasts. Tessa looked down at her own B-cups and shrugged. While they weren't big, they were pretty, with perky pinky-brown nipples that loved being nibbled. Somewhere out there was a man who didn't care how big they were. It just hadn't been her no-good, cheating ex, Rick, despite his professions to the contrary.

"Come on Tessa, it will be fun. Paste on a smile and let's go." Becky made faces at Tessa in the mirror until she laughed.

Tessa's smile dropped away. "I'm not ready to date again," she warned her friend. "I get queasy just thinking about it. How could I not know that Rick was screwing around on me? I feel like such an idiot. I'm twenty-six, an adult. I should have seen the signs, we dated for three years. We were all but engaged and I didn't realize he had a tart on the side? His double-D secretary, after he claimed to prefer small breasts? Am I really that blind?"

Disbelief colored her voice. She shook her head and sighed. It still hurt that he had cheated.

Becky rested her hands on Tessa's shoulders and massaged them lightly. "You knew; you just refused to see it. Remember Christmas? Come on; he was suddenly sick and couldn't spend the day with you."

"That was weird, because he was fine on Boxing Day," Tessa admitted, leaning into her friend's relaxing massage. "I thought he would be sick for days. He said he had a horrible case of food poisoning."

"And he didn't want you to come over and play nurse. And, how many dates did he cancel at the last minute?" Stroking softly, she urged Tessa to relax.

"Damn." Tessa slapped her hands onto her legs. "And the fucking trips out of town." Closing her eyes, she took four deep breaths. "I knew. I just didn't want to admit it. Why didn't you say something?" She glared at her friend.

"You were happy. Blind, but happy and I trust you. I knew that you would figure it out yourself, eventually." Patting Tessa's shoulders lightly, she added, "Buck up, let's go have a couple of beers and a few laughs. I promise not to try to hook you up." She grinned and winked.

"No fix ups? No pressure?" When Becky nodded, Tessa added, "Pinky swear." She held out her baby finger.

*The Gift*

A barking laugh escaped Becky and she stuck out her baby finger. "Pinky swear? What are we, first graders?" They shook fingers and she dropped a kiss on Tessa's head. "You're as close to a sister as I've got and I just want to look after you, but I promise not to try to hook you up." She paused before adding, "At least for tonight. You will get over him." Becky handed Tessa some lip gloss.

# ABOUT THE AUTHOR

I'm Katie O'Connor. No, that's not my real name, just in case you wondered! (Laugh.) I live in Calgary, Alberta, Canada. I am a wife, a mother, and a grandmother. Life has never been better.

I have dabbled in writing since my university days. There is some part of me that drives me to create stories and write them down. It is impossible for me NOT to write. I think my head would explode if I kept all those ideas trapped inside. I even dream story lines. I have thought about keeping a notebook beside my bed so I can start writing the ideas down. But then again, maybe not, because some of those dreams seem like fabulous stories while I am dreaming, but are a little suspect on closer examination under daylight.

My mind is a very busy place and the ideas just keep on coming. I have to jot them down some place, so my laptop is full of partially completed stories and dozens of idea files. For me, the most difficult part of the writing process is choosing names. Recently I went through some old files looking for a particular story. I had ten heroines with the same first name. So much for being creative. Okay, maybe I need a baby name book.

I've tried my hand at writing poetry, science fiction, adventures and romance novels. But my passion is, and always has been erotica and romance. Weirdly, my romance stories tend towards sweet rather than erotic.

Here's hoping you have enjoyed reading this and that it jazzes up your sex-life because we all deserve to have a fabulous one!

# WHERE TO FIND KATIE

I love to hear from my readers. Please feel free to contact me and tell me how you felt about this story. Better still, write a review and post it on-line.

https://www.goodreads.com/KatieOConnor
Blog: http://katieoh.blogspot.com
Email: katieoconnorwrites@gmail.com
Twitter: Katie O'Connor @KatieOhWrites
http://www.amazon.com/author/katieoconnor
https://www.facebook.com/KatieOConnorWrites

Thanks for reading!

Made in the USA
Columbia, SC
19 May 2018